Language of Love

Port Provident: Home to Love

Kristen Ethridge

Chapter One

THE SUN'S LAZY DESCENT over the Gulf of Mexico began for the evening as Jake Peoples pulled the eviction notice from the glove compartment of his truck. Since he was already parked in front of El Centro por las Lenguas—which his rusty Spanish skills translated as "The Center for Languages"—it made the most sense to just serve the notice now.

The imminent passing of the Maximized Revenue Zones ordinance he'd shepherded through the City Council shortly after his return to town made Jake one step closer to convincing Port Provident that he could run his family's business. And once this building was demolished to make way for the sparkling pool to enhance the new Peoples Property Group condominium development, he'd be one step closer to convincing himself he wasn't the failure he had come to suspect he just might be.

When Jake turned the age-worn brass knob on the remodeled Victorian home's red front door, it didn't budge. Locked? No wonder this place was a nonprofit. He'd made mistakes in business, to be sure, but even he knew the first rule of running a company was you couldn't make money if the doors were closed.

He raised his fist and rapped on the solid wood.

After about thirty seconds of silence, the distinct sound of the lock turning broke through. A woman of average height stepped into the sliver of an opening.

"Can I help you?" Her brow furrowed across a forehead whose smooth complexion fell a shade lighter than the designer latte he'd polished off this morning.

Jake had faced judges, juries and his own father. He could easily face a schoolteacher. "I need to speak to Gracie Garcia."

"I'm Graciela Garcia de Piedra." Her consonants rolled together with a south-of-the-border accent.

"Jake Peoples." He extended his hand. "Peoples Property Group."

Instead of reaching to shake, her hands flew up and cupped over her mouth. The combination of the vulnerable reaction, combined with the oversized door, further dwarfed her stature. She looked as if she might blow away in a strong gulf breeze. "Oh no... I know the rent check was a few days late this month. It's been tight lately. I'm so sorry. It won't happen again."

The shock in her voice reverberated on his eardrums. Jake thought of the eviction notice waiting in his back pocket. She might have fainted if he'd held it out to her as soon as she opened the door. "I'm not here about that. I need to discuss the City Council's Maximized Revenue Zones proposal with you."

"I don't know what you're talking about, Mr. Peoples." The questioning wrinkles returned above the pair of liquid-chocolate eyes. "I teach classes at the same time as the City Council meetings, so I never have the opportunity to attend them. I know there are condominiums being put up next door, but I assumed they would be confined to that large corner lot they're already working on."

He shook his head briefly. Jake needed to break the gaze between them if he wanted to maintain his concentration. Gracie Garcia had the kind of dark eyes that a man—even a landlord here on business—could lose himself in. In his former career as a lawyer, no member of a jury pool ever gave him a stare that shook him like this.

"The City Council will soon be rezoning Gulfview Boulevard to make the most out of the areas in town that cater to our tourist-based economy. Nonprofit businesses, like yours, will need to move to new locations outside these zones. This property will be needed so we can add amenities like a swimming pool and a clubhouse, which will allow us to sell more units and, in turn, direct more tax dollars to the city."

"You're saying I need to close?"

Was there a language barrier between them? Maybe he'd gotten the wrong contact name. Maybe the woman with the magnetic stare was a student, not the owner. The name she'd given was a lot longer than just plain old Gracie Garcia.

"I didn't say anything about closing. Just moving."

"With all due respect, it's not that simple. I'm a nonprofit organization. I operate on a nonprofit's shoestring budget. If the council forces El Centro to relocate, I'll have to close my doors."

Well, she was certainly talking like the owner. Absently, he wondered why she gave a different name.

"Surely you can find additional funding. The Houston newspaper just did a story last week on unused grant money."

The woman nodded her head in understanding. Her eyes glazed over with sadness, but she didn't back down. She had guts; Jake had to give her that.

He didn't particularly like that his words hurt her, but he couldn't afford to get caught up in the emotions. This vote was nothing more than a necessary step in a business plan. Above all, Jake knew he had to remember why he'd come home to Port Provident in the first place. No more "bleeding heart" stuff, as his father used to derisively refer to Jake's past endeavors. Emotions and business did not make a successful combination, and Jake had returned to Port Provident to take steps at Peoples Property Group that would ultimately prove to a generation of naysayers that he could be successful.

"Can I come in for a few minutes so we can discuss this?" At least he would try to honor the promise he'd made to his friend sponsoring the ordinance, City Councilman Carter Porter. The City Council temporarily postponed their vote until affected businesses could be notified and given a chance to adapt. By meeting the owner of El Centro personally right now, Jake could report back to Carter that the box had been checked. That way there could be no more delays.

She shook her head. "You've caught me at a bad time. I have a class tonight that I need to finish preparing for."

"Okay, Ms. Garcia. Best of luck with your school. Here's the official lease termination paperwork, which will be effective once the City Council passes the measure at their next meeting." He reached in his back pocket and pulled out the document, then something made him pause.

Jake couldn't get the name discrepancy out of his head. He needed to be sure he'd just lowered the boom on the right person. It wouldn't look good if he'd delivered the message to someone else by mistake. "You are the owner of this school, right? You're Gracie Garcia?"

She nodded. "Yes, why?"

"I thought you'd said something else a few minutes ago. Wasn't your last name longer?"

"My name is Graciela Garcia de Piedra. In the Mexican culture, children often have the surnames of both parents. The father's surname comes first, and then the mother's—but children go by their father's last name. So I go by Garcia. It makes things simpler. Do you know much about our culture and language, Mr. Peoples?"

"No." He raked his free hand through his hair. "I'm afraid I don't."

"Then maybe you don't understand just why this school is important and what the impact is of what the City Council is trying to do," Gracie said with a soft, yet deliberate clip to each syllable of her quiet words. She took the offending paperwork from Jake's hand, then slowly closed the door. The rasp of the turning lock brought a clear end to their encounter.

Jake turned to head back to his car, feeling uncomfortable about the message he'd just delivered, even though he knew he had no other option. The passage of the City Council resolution was key to finalizing Port Provident's newest condo development. The project was key to his remaining at the helm of Peoples Property Group. And remaining CEO of his family company was key to restoring his reputation in his hometown.

The less time he spent at El Centro por las Lenguas, the better. His grandmother was being honored at a Port Provident Historical Society dinner this evening, and he didn't want to miss her big night.

As he pushed the button that unlocked the truck's doors, he heard the crunch of gravel under feet behind him. Two fingers tapped lightly on his shoulder. Jake turned and saw Gracie's eyes first, silently pleading with him. Her pupils flared wide, crowding out the brown velvet coloring. He could see the fear within.

He hoped she couldn't see fear in his own eyes. Fear that the City Council wouldn't give him what he needed to just get on with his life and not feel the cloud of failure hanging heavily on his shoulders.

"You said you didn't know much about my students and their heritage—where they come from and why they're here. More than three hundred members of this community have come through my doors in the last five years to better their English skills. I don't provide the city with tax dollars myself, but my students do make an impact every day." Her voice halted.

Jake turned. The gulf breeze gently stirred her hair around to caress her cheek. It appeared to be almost the same deep color as her eyes.

"The ordinance is passing in a few days' time. I'm not a City Council member. I can't stop them from voting on it," he said. "The measure would have passed today except that your representative wanted to give you some time to find an alternate arrangement."

"You said this proposal will maximize revenue for the tourist sector of our local economy, right?" Her eyes locked straight on his, like a magnet pulling to a pole.

"That's the goal, yes," Jake nodded.

"Many of my students work in tourist-related jobs, such as our hotels and restaurants. A skilled labor force is just as important to our city as tax revenue. I believe we can't have the latter without the former. Can you stay for my class in half an hour and see for yourself what I do here?"

Giving Gracie a few more minutes wasn't going to change anything, but it would probably make everyone involved feel as if he'd done his due diligence. It might also alleviate the nagging feeling in the back of his mind that something about what he'd told Gracie Garcia just wasn't right. But family duty called.

"I already have plans for this evening, Ms. Garcia."

"Then I'm afraid you won't see what a big mistake you're making for the citizens of this community until it's too late." Gracie headed back toward the center. She had some pluck. He recognized it because he used to have some, too.

Back before he lost everything.

When the City Council met next week and the inevitable happened, Jake hoped that Gracie didn't lose the determined spring in her step. The world didn't need another jaded former business owner.

BEFORE JAKE COULD OPEN the door to get back in the truck, his cell phone rang. "Jake Peoples."

"Jake, it's Mitch." The wind whipping up over the nearby water made it a little difficult to hear his brother-in-law's voice. "Where are you? Jenna's panicking."

"Tell Jenna I'm on my way. I'm just wrapping up a meeting."

"Who are you meeting with?" After meeting Jake's sister Jenna in college and marrying her, Mitch Carson joined Peoples Property Group and now served as the chief financial officer. Jake had much to prove to others at the office, but not

Mitch. His brother-in-law was doing everything he could to help Jake during this transition.

"Graciela Garcia de Piedra. She owns the school located in the building at Nineteenth and Gulfview."

"Oh, you mean the rental property you want to tear down so the new condos will have a pool that'll compete better with Goodman's new project?"

"That's the one. Just making sure that the council vote can go forward. I figured it was best to get it out of the way ASAP."

"Hey, wasn't her rent late again this month? If she's that disorganized, maybe you're doing her a favor. She'd probably go out of business anyway." Mitch chuckled. "Your sister just walked up. We'll see you when you get here."

"Bye."

The phone call disconnected, and Jake couldn't help but think about Mitch's last sardonic statement. Mitch was right. Gracie obviously had some issues running her business. Better that she quit while she could instead of being forced into bankruptcy. The way Port Provident's economy kept growing, she could easily find another job—a real job with a steady paycheck—in no time.

Jake saw two people headed toward him. Neither one was Gracie, but he felt certain he'd seen both of these individuals before.

"Mr. Jake?" The first man regarded Jake skeptically and stopped in his tracks about ten feet away. "Can we help you? Is something wrong at one of the buildings?"

Jake hesitated to answer. "No, no problem with any of the buildings,"

"Oh, good, sir. Juan and me, well, we weren't sure why you'd be at *El Centro* unless you were looking for someone."

Juan. Jake nodded his head with dawning recognition. The man on the left was Juan Calderon, the head of landscaping for Peoples Property Group. And the one speaking to Jake was Pablo Morales, head of maintenance.

"I had a meeting with the owner of the school. Just taking care of some business. Enjoy your class tonight." He opened the door to his truck and climbed inside as his two employees headed for the door of the school. Jake wondered what they'd say to Gracie when they got inside, but he knew he had nothing to hide about his motives for being here.

GRACIE PLAYED HIDE-and-seek as she placed two fingers between a couple of slats of the mini-blinds covering the window in her office. Through the space she'd created, she could search the parking lot without being seen herself.

She knew of the Peoples family's reputation in Port Provident, but Jake himself didn't look that tough. With sandy blond hair and square shoulders, he looked less like a hard-edged executive and more like one of the surfers who hung out down by the Memorial Hotel waiting to catch a wave.

"Is he still out there?" Her sister Gloria's whisper brought more reminders of childhood, when they shared secrets in hushed tones.

The parking lot had begun to fill for the evening's classes and Gracie could see the vehicles of several regular students. The truck that had parked in the very first space, however, had already left, leaving behind a trail that seemed to perfectly illustrate Gracie's dreams for her school—a cloud of dust, disappearing into nothing.

"No, he's gone."

"People like him make me so mad," Gloria said through gritted teeth. "Remember when you used to date David and he tried to stop you from opening this school? Now, here's another mover and shaker in the community trying to push you around. They're all the same on that side of the tracks. They'll do whatever they want and not care about people like us."

Gracie didn't want to remember the past, but Gloria was right. "Ugh. Don't remind me. Why is running a business such a constant battle? I'm trying to help people live their dreams, the way Miss Martin helped me so many years ago by teaching me English when we first came to America. She helped me to do everything I could to reach my potential. I just want to do the same for others. It shouldn't be this hard to do the right thing."

"Well, what are you going to do? I couldn't help but overhear." Gloria stopped arranging the evening's books and materials.

"I don't know, Gloria. How do I fight the City Council?" Gracie nibbled on the nail of her pointer finger, a sign of nervous thinking she'd had since childhood.

The sound of footsteps outside the open office door shook Gracie out of her stunned condition.

"City Council? Why don't you call Pastor Ruiz's aunt, Angela, for help? She's our representative." Pablo Morales stopped near where Gracie stood. "Remember, Juan, when she helped you with that property tax issue a few months ago?"

"Oh, *sí*. She got it fixed *muy rapido*. Only took one phone call. I still have her number right here." He pulled out a small black cell phone and punched a few buttons, then handed it to Gracie. "There. It's dialing."

Gracie tried to take a deep breath, but there wasn't any time. Angela Ruiz answered on the second ring. Gracie didn't even know where to begin. She still felt as though her world had been turned upside down. This building was her home and her school. And now she'd just received eviction papers, pending a City Council vote.

"Hi, Councilwoman Ruiz. This is Gracie Garcia at *El Centro por las Lenguas* on Gulfview Boulevard." She tried to force as much normalcy in her tone of voice as she could. "Jake Peoples from Peoples Property Group just stopped by and handed me an eviction notice, effective once the vote passes at the next meeting. Is this vote a foregone conclusion?"

"He did what?" The councilwoman's volume level escalated and Gracie had to pull the phone back from her ear. "Carter Porter assured me that Jake Peoples—your landlord—would work with you personally to make new arrangements. You were not supposed to be pushed out the door. I asked for the vote to be postponed out of respect for the work that you and a few other affected nonprofits do. Let me make a few phone calls. I'll be at *El Centro* as soon as I can."

The phone call disconnected, leaving Gracie as confused as before. Maybe when the councilwoman arrived, things would become clearer. But for now, she still had a class to teach. She walked the short distance from her office to the classroom.

"Okay, class. Let's get to work." She didn't completely know how she was going to take on the City Council and the leader of one of the city's oldest developers, but for the next hour, she knew she just had to focus on what she did best—teaching students.

A knock on the building's front door interrupted Gracie as she wrapped up the day's lesson. "Just a moment, class. Keep practicing your dialogues with your neighbor."

As she walked down the hall, trepidation gripped Gracie's heart. The last time she answered a knock at the door—only a few hours ago—she'd been unwillingly pushed onto the battlefield in order to save her school. What now?

"Hi, Gracie." Councilwoman Angela Ruiz stood on the front porch. Behind her stood a woman Gracie recognized—Patti Cortez, a local reporter from KPPT-TV. "I brought along a friend of mine. This wasn't what Carter Porter promised me would happen when I agreed to consider his proposal. I told him that he couldn't expect my vote unless the companies would help businesses like yours move to areas outside these new zones. And clearly, that's not happening."

Gracie stepped aside, speechless at Angela Ruiz's quickly marshaled support. "Come on in. I'm just finishing up a class, but you can wait in my office, if you'd like."

Angela and Patti stepped inside, followed by a cameraman. "I want to get a story on tonight's newscast. We need to let the people know this proposal is out there and let them tell their council members if they think it's a good idea or not. That's what good government is—the will of the people," said the councilwoman as she came inside.

Gracie saw a white van painted with the KPPT-TV logo in the middle of the parking lot, with a round satellite dish on a pole pointed at the sky. "Ms. Garcia, do you mind if my cameraman shoots some footage of you with your class? We can use it as B-roll in the story." The reporter poked her head around the corner and looked in the classroom.

This was really happening. El Centro would be on the news tonight. People all over Port Provident would be able to hear her plea for themselves. "If it's okay with my students, it's okay with me." Every head in the classroom was already turned toward the door. No more dialogues were being practiced. Clearly, everyone wanted to know what was going on. Angela Ruiz stepped in the room.

"*Holá*, everyone. Gracie and I need your help. There is a proposal in front of City Council right now that may mean the end of El Centro. I'm sure most of you have seen Patti Cortez on TV. If you'd like to be part of a story to help save businesses like El Centro, could you stay for a few minutes after class tonight?"

Heads nodded. The unanimous show of support bolstered Gracie's confidence, which had been plummeting ever since Jake Peoples showed up on her doorstep. She took a deep breath, as she exhaled, she smiled for the first time in hours. She'd always supported her students. Gratitude overwhelmed her as she realized they were supporting her in turn.

"Thank you, everyone. I'm going to step into my office for just a second while the TV crew sets up, and then we'll do this as quickly as possible." Gracie's words came straight from a grateful heart. "Councilwoman Ruiz, while we're waiting, could you give everyone an overview of what the proposal before the City Council is, exactly?"

Angela nodded and began to explain as Gracie retreated to the safety of her office to collect her thoughts. "What's going on out there, *hermana*?"

Gloria set a textbook down on Gracie's desk. "All of a sudden, everyone seemed to be talking at once." A midwife at the birth center near Provident Medical Center, Gloria was escaping from the hustle and bustle of the center and using the quiet of Gracie's office to prepare for some upcoming continuing education classes.

Gracie leaned against the closed office door and gave her nail a good, nervous chew. "I want to pinch myself, Gloria. A TV crew is here to do a story on saving *El Centro*. Angela Ruiz brought them."

"A story on the news—about *El Centro*? Well, that's nothing short of a miracle."

Gloria was right. The developers and council members supporting this crazy proposal would have to take notice. A smile began to work up the corners of Gracie's mouth. This felt like a plan, a concrete plan to show Jake Peoples just what *El Centro por las Lenguas* meant to real people in the Port Provident community.

Her school—her livelihood, her mission—would still be open until the City Council's next meeting. And in that time, she just had to show the man who actually owned her building that this proposal he supported was a bad idea, one that would cause Gracie to lose everything she'd worked years for.

"Jake Peoples and others like him who think nonprofits should just be moved off into a dusty corner need to see they're wrong. They need to see the faces of the people whose lives are changed by the work done by nonprofits." She could hear her voice becoming louder as her heart filled with passion for her school. "People who share the same dream Mamí and Papí had when they made the decision to come to America and give our whole family the chance at a better life. They sacrificed for me, and I want to repay that sacrifice by doing the same for others."

Gloria stood and gave her sister a hug. "Then you have to make the most of this opportunity. You have to let the people of Port Provident know why you matter."

Gracie knew the fight for *El Centro* promised to be a David-and-Goliath type of struggle. Thinking of it in those terms, though, made Gracie pause. It tempered her fighting spirit and scared her all over again.

She didn't have even a slingshot to wield. Jake Peoples was a BOP, local slang for "Born on Provident." Born on this island into one of the oldest families in town, he carried a birthright of privilege. And obviously members of the local government were just waiting to do his company's bidding.

When Gracie Garcia came into the world in a rural hospital in Mexico, she had a blue collar instead of a rattle. What was she thinking? In Port Provident, Texas, Jake Peoples wasn't just any man, he held a pedigree of royalty.

How could a working-class woman change the heart of a king?

"*Lo necesito...*" Gracie said, her voice barely over a whisper.

"What do you need, *hermana*?"

"I don't know, Gloria. I need..." Air rushed from Gracie's lungs in fear as she faced the reality ahead. She'd never been on TV before. She'd never had her home and livelihood threatened like this before. How could she do the work that needed to be done when she didn't even know where to begin?

"You need prayer." Gloria stood and walked to her sister, then took her hand and held on tight as she began to speak.

Gracie felt taller and stronger as her sister's words poured over her. "Thank you. I feel as if maybe I can fight this battle. You've made me feel as if I'm not in this alone."

"You're not, *hermana*." Gloria still held tightly to her sister's hand and squeezed again. "I've had your back since you were born, Graciela." Gloria placed an arm around Gracie's shoulders and squeezed. "*Somos familia.*"

JAKE WALKED UP THE stairs at the Port Provident Garden Club, the scene of tonight's Historical Foundation awards dinner. He grimaced as he remembered being dragged to numerous functions here while growing up. Members of his family had been attending events at this place, the most exclusive club on the island, since it opened. Even so, Jake never felt as if he belonged here, because he never felt as if he belonged at any place that welcomed his father with open arms.

A chill ruffled the back of his neck, even though the weather felt like early summer. Jake never fully knew why his father's presence always made him uncomfortable, but at places like this, he still felt a nagging reminder of the icy coldness that had defined their father-son relationship.

Some things never changed, apparently. His father had died several months ago, but returning to Port Provident's most exclusive dinner club made a chill of self-doubt run down his spine, and he hadn't even run into a single person he knew yet.

"Jake!" Jenna waved her arms high above her head. Catching his eye, she waved him over to a table near the podium at the front. So much for his desire to lay low and not stir up any memories of his father in this old place. Slowly, he made his way to the space his sister had set aside for him.

Nana greeted him first, with a warm kiss on the cheek. "I'm so glad you were able to make it tonight, Jakey. Tonight wouldn't have been as special without you here."

"I wouldn't have missed your big evening for anything, Nana. You've done a lot of good work for a lot of people over the years through the Peoples Family Foundation. I am so proud to see your life's work recognized by this community." He admired how his grandmother used generosity and a giving spirit to make sure countless citizens had better lives.

"Jake...you're not going to believe this." Mitch grabbed his brother-in-law by the arm. "You've got to come with me."

"Mitch, what are you talking about?" Jake tried to make sense of why he was being led from the banquet hall like a show pony. "The dinner's about to start. Where are we going?"

"The lobby. There's a TV down there. You have to see what's on TV."

"But Mitch..." Jake's head spun, far beyond confused, as the pair walked down the stairs. "I don't even watch TV. You know that. I don't want to miss Nana's award."

His brother-in-law turned a corner, then stopped short, causing Jake to trip over his own feet. "You don't want to miss this, either." He pointed at the large TV on a pedestal in front of them both. Councilman Carter Porter also stood riveted to the screen.

Jake did a double take. On the screen was the same face framed by chocolate-brown hair he'd thought about during the entire drive to the Port Provident Garden Club. City Councilwoman Angela Ruiz flanked Gracie Garcia on the left, and the ESL teacher stood surrounded by at least fifteen other people. One held a sign. He locked his gaze on the words painted in red letters. "Save *El Centro*!"

"Turn the volume up." Jake's words came out sounding more like a bark than a request. He'd been wrong to question Mitch earlier. This definitely qualified as must-see-TV. It also qualified as the opening shot of a war over Gulfview Boulevard. How could Gracie have done this to him? He went to her school today to talk face-to-face. And this is how she repaid him? Public protests on a local newscast?

"Carter, what is going on here?" Jake spoke to his friend without looking in his direction. "I thought you said Angela Ruiz was onboard as long as I personally explained things to the owner of the school. I thought you were supposed to be helping me get through this."

"I am helping you, Jake. I brought your proposal before the City Council. I had enough votes lined up before Ruiz started asking questions. She's just new and trying to prove herself. Things will work out. Remember the district championship football game our senior year? You threw that pass with just a few seconds left. It started to pop out of my hands, but then I locked it down and ran it into the end zone." Carter clapped a palm of camaraderie on his former teammate's shoulder. "This is the same thing. We've been friends for a long time. I've never given up on you, even when you went to Austin. Don't worry, I'm going to score another touchdown with you on this one."

Carter's reminder reassured him. Gracie's little stunt would not keep him from the game-winning score Jake needed in order to ensure the success of the condominium project that would, in turn, ensure his confirmation as permanent CEO of Peoples Property Group.

This was now war. Gracie Garcia's students might be waving homemade signs of white posterboard on television tonight, but Jake promised himself that before the next City Council meeting, they would be waving the white flag.

Chapter Two

"YOU'RE NOT GETTING much work done, big brother." Jake swiveled his chair around. When did Jenna walk into his office? "I didn't hear you come in."

"I noticed. You've been leaning back in that overstuffed recliner you call a desk chair, just looking out the window at all the other office buildings downtown. I walked by earlier to have lunch with Mitch, but his conference call ran long. You haven't moved for at least five minutes." She walked around and perched on the edge of Jake's desk. "Something wrong?"

"No. Just thinking about the condo project." He couldn't tell his sister he'd really been thinking about Gracie Garcia. Ever since he'd seen her on TV last night, she'd consumed his thoughts with the determination in her words and the flash in her liquid chocolate eyes. He respected her determination, even though it caused him problems. If he could figure out what made her tick behind those flashing eyes, maybe he could solve this issue with her sooner.

"I heard you talking with Mitch about it at dinner last night. Don't you two ever take a break?" She gave Jake a playful closed-fist punch to the shoulder.

"Jenna, I can't take a break. I decided to finally join the family company in order to prove that you and Nana can depend on me, no matter what our father always said. I know

I'm not who he told everyone I was—and now I have to prove it to everyone else in this town."

He'd tried to get off the treadmill, to do something different. And look where that had gotten him. Right back to the same corner office, where he now had to work twice as hard—with no breaks—in order to make up for the one break that cost him almost everything. "Do you really think Dad, Grandfather and Great-Grandfather would approve if I took breaks from the company with their name on the door? With *our* name on the door?"

Jenna's blond ponytail bounced as she stood and folded her arms across her chest. Her stiff body language made her seem even taller than her usual inch under six feet. "Jake, lighten up. I didn't mean it like that and you know it. You've been so touchy since you moved back. You couldn't even enjoy Nana's big moment last night."

Jenna could stand there all she wanted with her arms crossed in disapproval. Jake could see he'd set off a little fuse in her. Did all women just stop speaking to him when they got mad? First Gracie, now his sister. Hopefully, Jenna wouldn't be contacting any reporters.

"I don't have the opportunity to be soft, Jenna. Too many people depend on me to make the right decisions and then execute them. That's business. People who listened to our father think I can't do this. But I have to prove them wrong. I'm a businessman."

"Well, I liked you better when you were just my brother. Those years in Austin changed you."

She had no idea. He'd tried and, still, he'd failed.

Just as his father always said he would. He knew that successfully leading this company would go a long way toward showing he wasn't the wayward son, doomed to failure, that everyone assumed him to be.

However, he'd learned a lesson—one he hoped sweet, idealistic Jenna never had to learn. If the family business failed, Jenna's husband would lose his job, too. Jenna and Mitch would get hurt. Nana would get hurt.

Jake could stomach the hurt that came with folding up his law practice. But he couldn't bear the thought of letting his mistakes affect the people who'd always loved and supported him.

"I'll always be your brother, Jen. But I have just a few more days to get the condo development plans in place so I can show the board that I am the right person to run this company."

"I don't know why you're so worried. Of course they'll approve your position. You're John Edward Peoples IV. The only other presidents of this company have been John Edward Peoples I, II and III. It's silly that you think they'd change more than a hundred years of tradition just because you spent a few years in Austin trying to practice law instead of working here with Daddy."

If only Jenna knew the real reason he'd stayed away from Port Provident all these years. Jenna had never felt the icy stare of their father's gaze. She'd never felt like an outsider in her own childhood home. She'd never lost her faith in the supposed unconditional love of a family. She'd never returned as a penniless prodigal, living on charity in her grandmother's carriage house, just to prove years of rumors wrong.

If only he had Jenna's faith in himself. In anything.

"We'll see, Jenna. For now, I'm late." Jake plucked his cell phone off the charger on the desk and reached for his keys. He didn't have a meeting on the calendar, but it was long past time to keep dwelling on old memories. He needed to check up on the condo project. The sales office would be opening soon and Jake hadn't done a final walk-through.

"Okay. But before you go, Jake, promise me this." Among many other exceptional traits, Jenna stood almost six feet tall, and the not-so-little sister had no trouble looking her big brother straight in the eyes at his own six-feet-two. She paused, but didn't say anything. A few seconds passed, marked by the ticking of Jake's wall clock. "What, Jenna?" "Just don't lose sight of what's really important."

"I DON'T UNDERSTAND how you can't even try to help me resolve this issue. I've been a tenant of yours for years."

As he walked down the hallway, Jake heard a raised voice. Usually the office was a quiet place— employees of Peoples Property Group spent a lot of time in the field, and when they were in the building, they all had plenty of work to keep busy.

"Ms. Garcia, I've already explained this to you." Mitch's voice sounded stressed. "Your lease has a clause for termination if the city's rules and ordinances change. It's all right there in black and white."

So, after her little stunt on TV last night, Gracie Garcia decided to come to the office? She might have been looking for sympathy on the evening news, but Jake knew she'd find none in this office.

"So that's it? When the City Council votes, you're going to give me forty-eight hours to move out of the place where I've lived and worked for almost six years? And you're not going to help me find someplace else to go?"

Jake stopped and stood in the office doorway. His adversary didn't sound quite so aggressive now.

"Ms. Garcia, in the last year, your rent check has been received at least one week past due six times. You're not exactly a model tenant." Mitch caught Jake's eye and waved him in. "Jake, you remember Ms. Garcia?"

"We've met. And I caught your television appearance last night." Jake chose to stay in the doorway. He knew a thing or two about angry women—best to keep a safe distance.

"Is that what this is about? The story on the news last night? You won't help me because I talked to the media about your proposal to the City Council?"

Jake shook his head. "Not exactly, but you didn't exactly win any fans here. And, as Mitch said, there have been some issues. This turn of events is best for everyone. We'll get what we need to finish our new development and you'll get out from under a lease you obviously can't afford."

She looked from Jake to Mitch, then back to Jake. Her chocolate-brown eyes pleaded with Jake to change his mind. "It's been a tough year, I won't deny that. But I've been a good tenant. And I should be getting some grant money soon that I will be using to create a new revenue stream. Things will be getting better. Soon. Can you please find me another place or at least give me a letter of recommendation?"

Jake remembered his own recent past, of needing to make a change and struggling with the available options. But he had to defer to Mitch on this. Clearly, Mitch knew the account, while Jake had only been back at the company for a handful of weeks. Jake needed to be the CEO of the company, not a micromanager. It was Mitch's call. Even if Jake didn't feel altogether right about the decision.

As one of Port Provident's largest companies, he would have figured there was some mercy Peoples Property Group could show. But that was probably his "bleeding heart" talking, as his father always said. It was time for Jake to grow up and act like a businessman. Like Mitch.

Jake decided to remain silent, even though he didn't necessarily want to. He wanted to make things better for Gracie Garcia and her molten chocolate eyes. He didn't like being the reason they were dull and filled with sadness right now.

Absently, Jake wondered what he could do to put a twinkle in them. He knew that with her petite features, Gracie would be pretty when she smiled. He wanted to see if his theory was correct—but how?

Mitch cleared his throat, bringing Jake back to reality.

"No, Ms. Garcia, I'm sorry. We just can't," said Mitch, closing the folder containing Gracie's lease and other paperwork.

A CLASS ON TIME MANAGEMENT once taught Gracie to structure her day's plans in order of importance. After her last-ditch effort at the Peoples Property Group office this morning clearly failed, she had to come up with a new game plan. From now until the next City Council meeting, the only item on her calendar looked the same: find a way to save *El Centro.*

She expected her last, best hope to arrive at her post office box soon. A letter notifying the Gulf Coast Educational Foundation grant recipients about their upcoming grants should have been mailed last week, which meant it would arrive any day. If she postponed the GED program she wanted to start, the grant would give *El Centro* enough money to help Gracie secure a new location—without any help from Jake Peoples or his coldhearted company.

A truck pulled into the parking lot. After yesterday, she'd recognize it anywhere. It pulled past her, then turned around before driving to the dirt lot a block away. Just what she'd expect from Jake Peoples. He'd do whatever he wanted, and never notice the people on the sidelines.

"Miss Gracie!" Pablo Morales's voice carried across the parking lot. He stood next to Juan, and both waved enthusiastically in her direction.

It took a few minutes for her to cross the entire lot. Her shoes crunched the gravel under her feet, making a satisfying sound as she walked toward the small group. Grinding, staccato. The perfect complement to her mood. Every step seemed to build her resolve to give Jake the piece of her mind she didn't have the courage to give while she stood in the Peoples Property Group office.

"We were talking with Mr. Jake about *El Centro,*" Pablo stepped back so Gracie could join their circle of conversation. Her shoulder brushed Jake's forearm as she walked up. The starched cotton of his sleeve felt cool on her arm.

"If you want to know what the school is really about, Mr. Jake, you should come visit a class. We both missed class last week due to work, so we'll both be up here tonight for a makeup session. You should join us," Juan said.

"And if you want to see how the school has changed the community, you should really come up to our church tomorrow night for the Wednesday service," Pablo continued. "Most of the members of the church have worked with Gracie in one way or another."

Jake cleared his throat. "Thanks for the invitation, but I don't really think that's necessary."

"Did you hear us on TV last night? We said this school benefits you because it benefits us. You can meet our families and friends and see how they benefit, too." Juan joined in, leaning on a shovel almost as tall as Gracie herself. "The school isn't just about the lessons. It's about building a community."

Gracie gave a reflexive nod. Juan was right. Her school provided more than just books and lessons. But what would Jake care? His business card might read *Developer*, but all he appeared to want to do was tear things down.

The sun shone brightly in Gracie's eyes, causing her to squint. Through her eyelashes, she could see Jake's eyebrow rise and a corresponding shoulder shrug.

"I'll see." Jake's voice sounded distant, as though he spoke to someone else.

"Where's your church?" Gracie's jaw dropped open in shock. Then she spoke without thinking. "On Fifty-First Street, three blocks west of Broadway. The service starts at five-thirty."

What was she doing? She'd just given Jake Peoples directions to their church, so he could further infiltrate her life.

How could she confront him now? She couldn't very well tell off someone who said he was thinking about joining her and her students at church. What kind of witness would that make her?

He moved on without another word and looked back at a small pink building where Juan and Pablo had been working. "I want to take a quick walk-through of the condo sales office. I'll need to sign off on the project before we open it up this weekend."

"This weekend? What do you mean?" Gracie said, looking quickly between Jake and the structure at the end of the parking lot, then back to Jake as he answered. "We're going to start staffing our sales office for the condo project this weekend. It's almost the start of summer and we want to be able to sell units at prebuild prices to people while they're here on vacation."

The flame inside Gracie that was just barely simmering after the church discussion now bubbled up to a rapid boil. "Have you no shame? Angela Ruiz said you're supposed to be trying to help *El Centro*. Now I find out you're moving full steam ahead on bulldozing my home and my school before the City Council even holds a vote? You never intended to help me or my school, did you? You lied to the City Council."

"I did not, Gracie. I met with you personally at your school to deliver the news, exactly as I told Councilman Porter I would. Apparently, there was a misunderstanding between your representative and mine. But I never said I was going to stop our project. It doesn't make any sense for my company to put the condos on hold while we wait for a decision."

The hairs on the back of Gracie's neck stood up. His reply came across so arrogantly. Exactly as she'd expected.

She needed him to slow down and provide some kind of assistance, just as Angela Ruiz had assured her he would. She didn't have much time or many options otherwise. What would get Jake's attention? What could she say to make the big bad businessman not see her little school as necessary collateral damage?

Help me to see this situation as you see it, Father. Help me to know what I should do.

Jake wordlessly turned and began to walk toward the sales office. Pablo and Juan followed behind their boss.

"Mentor me."

Jake stopped and looked over his shoulder at her. His expression, one eyebrow raised, one lowered, gave his answer without a word. Gracie could see it on his face. He thought she was nuts.

Well, maybe so.

Nuts about her school. Crazy about her students. She would do anything to save *El Centro*. She'd even throw herself at Jake Peoples's feet.

She knew she needed a bold idea to save her school.

Maybe she just needed a way for Jake to see that her school was more than documents in a folder at Peoples Property Group.

Gracie always felt proud of what she'd accomplished in building El Centro. It filled the need in her soul to help others. She took pride in what her students accomplished because of the lessons they'd learned there.

But if she didn't make Jake see her school as valuable, next week all she'd have left was her pride.

Surely she hadn't just asked him to be her business mentor.

Not only did he not have the time, he wasn't about to step in and solve someone's problems. Again.

"No. I can't."

"No, you can't?" Gracie threw him a sideways glance. "Or no, you won't?"

"Does it really matter? No still means no, either way." Jake could barely explain his reasons to himself beyond the fact that he wasn't taking on anything in his life right now that wasn't a sure thing. This condo project was his shot to prove years of gossip wrong and he would allow nothing—not even a determined teacher with a molten-chocolate gaze—to stand in his way.

She took three big steps, stopping so close he could smell her perfume. Floral, with a hint of baby powder. A delicate scent, but her defiant posture showed that Gracie Garcia was not a shrinking rose.

"Yes, it does. I was told you gave your word to help me. I've now asked for your help. If you can't help me, that's one thing." She met his eyes with a straight stare. The irises of her eyes deepened in color from cocoa to the finest dark chocolate. "But if you just *won't* help me, well, then, you don't understand what's important in this life."

Her words struck him like a punch to the gut. Wasn't that almost exactly what Jenna had told him earlier? That he needed to remember the important things in life?

Nothing in his life had priority over securing his family's future. The most important thing was being named permanent CEO of Peoples Property Group.

That meant coming up with a solution to the problem presented by Gracie Garcia, not finding her a lifeboat. She wouldn't understand it, but he had to keep himself from drowning right now.

"You don't know me well enough to tell me what I do or do not understand." He roughed up a couple of pebbles under the sole of his shoe, standing his ground. "I understand that I have a business to run. And I understand I have a school to get out of my way so I can get a swimming pool for a condominium built in time to make my board of directors happy." Frustration forced the words out of Jake's mouth before he had a chance to think through what he was saying.

"Oh." Her hand flew over her mouth, cutting off any further reply. She stared at him, eyes wide as the harvest moon that would sometimes hang low over the nearby Gulf of Mexico. And then, in her eyes, Jake saw the faintest accumulation of moisture begin in the corners.

"Gracie, I'm..."

"No, you're not." Even as close as they stood to one another, he could barely hear her whisper.

Jake reached out and placed his hands on her arms, then quickly dropped them. As his palms brushed over Gracie's bare skin, he noticed that she felt cold, in spite of the sunshine overhead. He shouldn't have touched her—he only wished he could reach out and steal back his chilling words. But he couldn't. Besides, he'd only spoken the truth. This whole situation came down to nothing more than a business deal. It wasn't personal.

But the look in Gracie's eyes, now brimming with tears, told him she viewed things as extremely personal.

"Gracie," Jake started. He didn't intend to be anyone's business mentor, but he could teach her, right now, that his actions had to do with his obligations to his job and nothing more.

"No, Jake. I don't want to hear some fancy words you learned in a class for your MBA. When you hear P&L you think of a profit and loss sheet. I think of people and love." She stepped back, putting more distance between the two of them. "I have to go to the post office. My fight for my students isn't over. Keep your fancy schools and big-time degrees. You're the one who needs to be taught a thing or two."

Gracie squared her shoulders, still dotted with gooseflesh, and walked away with all the stoicism of a soldier on the front lines.

"So, first she asks me to be her mentor, then she says she wants to teach me a lesson," Jake mused out loud, more to himself than the other two men. "Is she crazy, or something else?"

"Oh, she's something, all right, Mr. Jake." Juan nodded his head. "You'll see."

Chapter Three

AFTER THE CONFRONTATION with Gracie, Jake wrapped up his afternoon by checking out some new land at the east end of Provident Island. It took him about twenty minutes to drive back into town, but Jake didn't mind.

Driving the two-lane strip of highway that ran parallel to the beach always soothed his soul. Watching the sun sparkle on the gentle rolls of surf, he noted to himself with irony that if he wound up buying and developing the property he'd just surveyed, he'd eventually be responsible for ruining the peace and quiet he'd always loved.

His cell phone rang, and Jake pulled over to answer it so he could watch the waves as he talked. Even though his task list for the week overflowed with to-dos, he wasn't in a hurry to get back to his desk this afternoon. He needed to think about some tasks looming on the horizon and push some other things—like Gracie Garcia—out of his mind.

"Jake, it's Carter. We have a problem."

What could possibly happen now? Since Carter all but assured Jake they had a done deal, Jake had watched a protest against his company on TV and been told by a pit bull of a teacher that he had a lesson to learn.

"Explain."

"I just got a visit at my office from Angela Ruiz. She's not happy with how things were handled with this little school. She told me she personally arranged that story we saw on KPPT last night and she's going to arrange more coverage featuring other constituents if we don't make this right. Jake, I'm going into an election this fall. I'm your friend and I want to see you succeed, but I can't afford to have this be a black mark on my reputation."

"So, last night's news story was her idea, not the teacher's?" Jake was surprised to hear that Gracie hadn't pulled that together. "What do you need me to do, Carter?"

"I'm getting calls left and right today from people wanting to know why I'm helping to close small businesses. You need to meet with that teacher again. Do something. And then we need a follow-up story that's more favorable to our side. Angela Ruiz wants to see you personally involved. Offer the teacher some help, business owner to business owner. Find a way for her to move, and you'll be a hero."

Great. Carter was asking him to be Gracie's business mentor. It figured.

Jake wrapped up the call and pulled back onto the quiet highway. That peaceful feeling he'd just had moments ago flew away like a seagull chasing a meal.

One more shot. Out of respect for Carter Porter and their friendship dating back to their school days, he'd give Gracie Garcia one more shot. He hoped sitting through one night of class would help him pass Angela Ruiz's test.

When he arrived, Juan and Pablo were just getting out of their cars.

"So, when does the class start?" Jake asked, tired of cooling his heels in a parking lot that felt more brimstone than balmy, even as the early Texas summer evening was setting in.

"About two or three minutes. Gracie will open the door as soon as she has everything ready to go. She takes good care of us," Juan replied.

A brief snort pushed through Jake's nose. He remembered Mitch's words earlier today about Gracie's organizational skills. Just as paying bills late wasn't a good sign for a business, taking good care of your clients never included leaving them waiting in a parking lot while you did last-minute preparations.

"Allergies, Mr. Jake?" Pablo looked at him, head tilted a little to one side.

Jake forced himself to focus. "What? Oh, no, not allergies."

"I know you've been away for a while, Mr. Jake, so you probably don't remember when I was hired at the company," Juan said. "Drug violence forced me to unexpectedly leave my home in Colombia. I knew some English, but not enough to get another job in a bank as I had back home, so I took a job as just another member of the landscape crew to support my family. By working with Gracie, I'm fluent in English. Now, I manage everything your company does to keep the properties looking great from the outside. In the middle of the night, I left everything behind in Colombia. But Gracie always believed in me and her work here at El Centro has helped me provide for my family here and keep others in my country safe."

Jake tried to take in all of Juan's story. He'd never realized that his good-natured employee had given up everything so his family would be safe from violence. Jake knew Juan was a hard worker. But he never realized how hard Juan had to work outside his job—here at El Centro—in order to secure his future. He never realized that a teacher in a small school could impact people around the world.

"Thanks for sharing that with me, Juan." Jake wanted to say more, but the sound of a clicking noise made Jake look over his shoulder.

The front door started to swing open. Before he could finish his conversation with his employees, the signal for class to start swept everyone inside.

Gracie stood in the doorway. Using only her feet, she struggled to push the doorstop in firmly enough to hold the heavy, oversized door open. Juan and Pablo walked past and Gracie leaned in as though she were whispering something.

"*Está bien*," Jake heard Gracie say as he stepped inside. "Now, sit. *Sientese*." She pointed toward the chairs in the room but laughed as she said the phrase.

It brought a musical tone to match the wide smile on her face. He wasn't one hundred percent sure what she'd just said, but the twinkle in her eyes made it hard to look away.

"Mr. Peoples," Gracie said, her smile dropping into an expression of shock as she noticed Jake. "What are you doing here?"

He shoved his hands into his pockets. With effort, he pulled his gaze downward for a split second. "I'm here to learn more about the school."

He couldn't say he was looking forward to the class or the work because, well, he wasn't. He was just doing what the City Council expected of him—an hour of due diligence to see what help could be offered. And he wasn't about to lie about it, even if the smile on her face dropped a few inches at the sound of his blunt statement.

Remember why you're here, Peoples, he reminded himself. *Just check this box, then report back to Carter so he can arrange a follow-up with KPPT-TV.*

"Um. Okay." She shook her head almost imperceptibly, then turned and started to walk away from the door and Jake. "The classroom's back here."

Just inside the door to the left was a set of closed French doors. He looked through the delicate glass panes into the dimly lit room, Jake could make out a desk with an older, boxy computer on top, as well as some filing cabinets. That must be Gracie's office. He looked past the "Private" sign hanging on the handrail of the staircase and assumed Gracie's own apartment took up the second floor of the renovated two-story house.

Jake didn't know exactly what he'd been expecting, but it wasn't this.

The whole building appeared well-kept. As the landlord, he could appreciate that. It seemed as if time and effort had not just been merely spent, but lavished, in order to make this area into a pleasant environment.

From hearing Mitch's earlier words, Jake never would have guessed that Gracie's school and home would look like this. He expected at least disarray, if not some form of chaos.

"If you'd like, you may sit there." She gestured to a blue plastic chair at the end of one of the middle tables. "Okay, everyone, go ahead and take your seats."

Gracie moved to the front of the room and began to write on the whiteboard with a red marker. She spelled out "FOOD" in clear, neat letters. "I know many of you work in restaurants, and for a number of you, the American dream means opening a restaurant of your own. That was the dream in my own family. My parents opened Huarache's Café shortly after we came from Mexico. I grew up in the restaurant and learned just what hard work in a great country can bring." Gracie nodded and made eye contact with three or four students. "In Beginning ESL, we learned basic words for food and what we do in the kitchen. Tonight, we'll practice our English by doing a few restaurant dialogues with a partner and writing our own restaurant menus."

Restaurant menus? Jake was no longer impressed. He could not believe his ears. This is what *El Centro* taught? Graciela Garcia de Piedra missed her calling. She should have opened an acting academy instead of an ESL school. She fooled her City Council representative into thinking *El Centro* served as some necessary educational center. Instead, here her students sat, writing restaurant menus.

"We also have a special guest tonight, local developer Jake Peoples." Gracie pointed in Jake's direction and he raised his hand slightly in acknowledgment.

A small chorus of "*Hola*" overlapped by "Hello" carried across the room. Some voices sounded quiet and shy, others seemed louder and more confident. Their teacher may have planned menu-writing as a lesson, but at least the students were friendly—even if Jake could clearly tell they weren't going to learn anything useful tonight.

"Okay, class, let's get started. Open your workbooks to page thirty-two." Gracie's slim fingers flipped the switch on an overhead projector and laid a transparency slide atop the glass plate.

Watching her hands, Jake noticed that all her nails appeared short. Studying them more closely, he could see that each was chewed down to where the white tip just barely peeked over the top of the pad on the finger.

Once the students appeared ready, she began the lesson with a review of basic food and cooking vocabulary. Then, the students broke up into groups of two in order to practice dialogues from the workbook. Jake watched as everyone else at his table paired off. He remained alone.

"Would you like to come work with us, Mr. Jake?" Juan gestured to an empty plastic chair beside Pablo. Jake nodded. He appreciated that Juan and Pablo tried to make him feel welcome.

Participating in the exercise seemed about as exciting as microwaving a bowl of soup. He checked his watch. He couldn't possibly stay for the whole class. The room quickly filled with the sounds of students talking to one another. Even though everyone seemed to be taking the assignment seriously, Jake noted with some surprise that every face he could see wore a smile. They appeared to enjoy the work.

He certainly couldn't remember any smiles in mock court back in law school. Or in his economics class while he earned his MBA. There weren't many professors at the University of Texas who brought anything other than a syllabus to class, certainly not personal relationships. But then again, there weren't many professors at one of the world's largest universities who would consider menu-writing a real lesson.

The only person not smiling was the teacher. Gracie's forehead furrowed as she noticed Jake in the corner chair. She didn't say a word, but just kept walking briskly past him, then disappeared behind a small door in the back corner of the room.

Jake nodded to himself as it clicked shut. Just as Mitch had said earlier, Gracie appeared to be in over her head. Before Jake ever set foot inside *El Centro*, he could see that. Judging by her nervousness tonight, his first impression turned out to be absolutely correct.

Really, there wasn't much more to observe about the center. Jake knew from a quick Google search that three churches on Provident Island provided small English as a Second Language programs. This school wasn't anything special. When *El Centro* closed, the students could still get help on their language skills elsewhere, Jake could have his condo development and Gracie Garcia could be freed of the financial burden of running this place.

Sitting through this class had so far proven not to be a good use of his time. There was only one more box to check: getting out of here as soon as possible in a way that would ruffle as few feathers as possible.

He could probably get Gracie a listing of local apartments to rent and recommend her for a job to the directors of those other ESL programs. Surely Nana had worked with at least one of them through the Peoples Family Foundation and would make an introduction. He'd brainstorm some details back at the office and let Carter— and Gracie—know in the morning.

As Jake stood, Juan and Pablo paused from looking up a word in the Spanish-English dictionary. "Did you change your mind about working with us, Mr. Jake?" Pablo asked.

"I think I've seen what I need to see for tonight."

"So, you like *El Centro, sí*?" Juan nodded at Jake. "I know Gracie has plans to do big things here. But she needs someone like you who can help her. We think it's great you're here."

"I'm only here because the City Council asked me to come see if there was a way to cause Gracie as little hassle as possible before Peoples Property Group finishes the new condo project on this land."

Juan shook his head. "El Centro's still going to close?"

"Next week, barring any further complications. I think it will work out in the end for everyone."

"Mr. Jake, you can't do that. This place is special." Worry settled across Juan's heavy brow. Pablo remained silent, looking down at the table.

"There are other ESL programs in town," Jake said. "That big church over on Fifty-Second Street offers classes. And they'd probably be happy to have Gracie's help."

"Mr. Jake, it wouldn't be the same. Gracie holds classes in the evenings for those of us who work during the day. She stays open on weekends and makes sure the classes are what all of us are looking for. She makes it personal." Juan pointed to the worksheets for the evening's lesson. "Most of the people here work for restaurants, so Gracie makes sure that there are a lot of lessons focusing on those things. She's created lessons just for Pablo and me, too."

"I appreciate that you both are taking the initiative to advance in your careers," Jake said. He admired their loyalty to the school, and the teacher who ran it. But the only thing that concerned Jake right now was showing the Peoples Property Group board of directors that he could indeed be trusted with his family's legacy.

"Mr. Jake," Pablo broke in. "We've said it before, but maybe you don't understand. This school doesn't just benefit us. It benefits you. Juan and I are better employees for you because of what we learn here."

Surprising himself, Jake sat down in the chair next to his head of maintenance. He remembered Juan's story about leaving Colombia in the middle of the night and coming to a country where he could barely speak the language. Jake himself knew something about starting over. In recognition of that kindred spirit, he knew he needed to invest five more minutes with two employees who were trying to be the best they could be.

CLEARLY, THERE HAD been no benefit in inviting Jake to come tonight. Gracie tried not to stare too obviously through lacy curtains covering the glass in the door connecting her office and the classroom.

Why was he just sitting there?

First, Jake spent most of his time sitting in the corner like a preschooler in time-out. Now, finally, he moved to a table with Pablo and Juan. Gracie wished she had some superpowers in order to hear the discussion through the walls of her office. But since that wasn't realistic, her only option seemed to quit acting like *un pollo grande.*

She had to stop being a big chicken. Curiosity finally got the best of her, and she opened the door and started toward the table.

Wait a minute. Wouldn't do to look too desperate.

Gracie turned and walked to a table a little further away first. "Hi, Patricia. Everything going okay?"

"Yes, Gracie. Laura and me, we're almost finished with our dialogue."

"Laura and I." She smiled as she corrected the common grammatical error, wanting to make her student comfortable. Patricia had elementary school-aged children and Gracie always tried to be sensitive to the fact that it could be awkward for Patricia, as an adult, to be learning many of the same language rules and lessons her children were being taught. "If you finish early, find a table to trade with and practice your dialogues with someone else."

Gracie consciously willed her feet not to move any quicker than normal while walking to Juan and Pablo's table. She badly wanted to know what was being said, but if things were as gloomy as they looked from the office, maybe ignorance was bliss.

"How's everything going here?" Gracie smiled at Juan and Pablo, but really meant the words for Jake.

"Miss Gracie, we're talking with Mr. Jake. We don't want to see the school close." Pablo laid Gracie's ultimate fear out on the table like the workbooks and dictionaries.

Apparently, Jake hadn't seen anything to change his mind.

The lump pushed its way up to the back of her throat. She would not allow them to see her cry. Pivoting on the balls of her feet, Gracie took off running for the office. Her shoes slid on the freshly waxed hardwood floor, skidding a little to the right, a little to the left.

Tears pooled in Gracie's eyes, blurring her vision. Breathe, Gracie reminded herself. Even though she knew that's what she should do, surges of adrenaline continued forcing their way through her veins and would not allow her to maintain a slow, calming breath pattern. Gracie exhaled as a hand pressed firmly on the small of her back.

"Come with me." Jake's low voice whispered into her ear.

His words caused the tap of embarrassment to open all the way.

Why him? Jake's hand stayed on her back. She could feel his fingers through the thin cotton of her shirt. Her stomach lightly fluttered as he steered her toward the door to the office. His free right hand reached out for the doorknob, swiftly turned it, and pulled back, ushering her into the office.

The door clicked behind them, separating them from the room full of students. The silence beat on Gracie's eardrums more loudly than the recent commotion. She needed to thank Jake for getting her out of the classroom but couldn't seem to speak. It was his fault that she found herself in the situation in the first place.

"Do you need to sit down?" Jake asked and walked around the room to Gracie's desk, then pulled out the chair.

Nodding, Gracie took a few steps and gratefully sat down. The hard plastic of the chair felt cold on her thighs. "I guess you have a nicer chair than this. Probably leather, right?"

"Yeah, it's leather. Why?"

Gracie craned her neck so she could look Jake in the eye. "I don't know. The thought just occurred to me."

Not too long ago, Gracie considered herself successful. *El Centro por las Lenguas* didn't carry debt and paid the bills every month, even though most months required some kind of juggling. There was little room for anything else, not even new furniture. Almost everything in her school was a hand-me-down.

In a matter of days, her dreams would be secondhand as well.

"I'll never have a fancy leather chair."

"Do you want one? I'm sure there's an extra one at my office somewhere."

"What would be the point? You'd just have to move it back after you shut me down." Gracie stood up. She felt licks of flames in her soul. Instead of worrying, she needed to be doing something. She didn't have any more time to waste in the office or with Jake Peoples. "Excuse me, Mr. Peoples."

Gracie hoped he could hear the determination in her voice. She kept her eyes lowered, because she knew if she locked on Jake's gaze, she'd lose her resolve. Even when they argued, his eyes always held a slightly mischievous gleam that made her lose her train of thought. And right now, she didn't want to think of Jake Peoples as boyishly attractive. She wanted to remember him as the stumbling block to her dreams. "I have classes to teach while I still have time to do so."

Chapter Four

AFTER A FULL WEDNESDAY in his office with spreadsheets, everything seemed fuzzy on the computer screen in front of Jake, but he'd pressed on. He would know these numbers backwards and forwards before the board meeting to confirm him as permanent CEO. Jake would not—no, could not—give the board any new excuses for denying him the job.

He looked down at nothing in particular, enjoying the feel of the muscles in his neck stretching. After a twelve-hour workday, maybe a change of scenery was in order. He could take his laptop home and look over more data tonight after dinner with his grandmother. At least the numbers had kept his mind off the situation with *El Centro*.

And Gracie Garcia. Jake allowed in the mental image he'd kept at bay all day. She looked like sweetness itself—with chocolate eyes and soft cocoa-powder hair, paired with honey-kissed skin.

But sugar and spice she was not. More like a personality of jalapeños and salsa. Gracie Garcia was all fire.

If they hadn't found themselves on opposite sides of this city council measure, Jake thought they might have been friends. He liked people with pluck. And Gracie had pluck by the pound.

He needed to keep his head on straight and get this project finished, but since he was alone with his thoughts, he didn't see too much harm in admitting he liked the ESL teacher's determination and chili-and-pepper sass.

Pulling his car out of the parking lot, Jake decided to take the long way home. Seeing the waves from Gulfview Boulevard would calm him. The cell phone lying on the passenger seat rang loudly. Still deep in thought, Jake picked up the phone and absently connected the call without taking his eyes off the road.

"Jake Peoples."

"Jake, it's Nana." A cheerful voice greeted him through the speaker. "Am I interrupting you?"

"No, not really. Just thinking through some things as I'm heading home. I always have time for you, Nana."

Diana Powell Peoples, chairman emeritus of the board of directors of Peoples Property Group and director of the Peoples Family Foundation, always commanded Jake's full attention. Not because of her titles. Because of the unconditional love she'd always shown him, even when his own parents treated him like a burden, like a stranger, even though he never knew exactly why.

"Sweet grandson." He could almost hear a smile in her words. "Listen, I won't keep you. I'm sure you're busy. I just wanted to tell you I've had something come up tonight and I can't make our usual Wednesday night dinner date."

"Oh. Well, that's okay, Nana." Jake tried to keep from sounding too disappointed. Since his return to Port Provident, he looked forward to his weekly dinners with Nana. "Next week?"

"Of course. And I'm sure I'll see you around before then. You do live in the carriage house behind my house." She laughed. "You can't get away from me."

"I wouldn't even think about trying to, Nana." He meant it.

His grandmother's welcome with open arms had stilled gossiping tongues after Jake moved back. It also had stilled his restless spirit after so many years of wondering what he'd done to reap such distance and cruelty from his father.

"I'll see you soon. Have a good night."

"I'll do my best. Love you."

Gracie Garcia's face kept popping into Jake's mind as he drove. He remembered the stern look on her face just before she left him in the parking lot and then again as she'd left him alone in her office.

He knew what she was. His adversary. The stumbling block to his future. A beautiful, determined woman who wouldn't leave him alone. Who wouldn't leave his thoughts...

He slowed the car for a red light and looked up. Fifty-First Street. Gracie Garcia's church was only a few blocks' drive away. And now his plans for the evening had been canceled. Jake tried not to agree with Juan's declaration in the parking lot that the ESL teacher was "something else." But Jake valued honesty, and knew he couldn't disagree, even if he wanted to.

Gracie *was* something else. And he needed to do something once and for all about the wrench she and her school had thrown in his business plans—and his thoughts.

Jake found the church easily. He couldn't see an available space in the parking lot, so he parked in front of a small white house about two blocks down the street. All the houses around the church looked similar in style, probably dating to just after World War II.

In spite of the intervening years, every house looked good as new—fresh paint, manicured lawns, sprinkles of flowers in beds lining sidewalks. A group of children played tag in a yard across the street. In more than thirty years of living in Port Provident, Jake had avoided coming to this side of town. But now, looking around, for the life of him, he couldn't understand why.

The sound of rapidly spoken Spanish reached Jake before he stepped up to the open front doors of *La Iglesia de la Luz del Mundo*.

"*Bienvenidos*." A man wearing a starched white guayabera reached out to shake Jake's hand. "I'm Marco Ruiz, the pastor. Can I help you find someone?"

"Jake Peoples." Jake extended his hand. "I'm looking for Juan Calderon or Pablo Morales. Are they here yet?"

"*Mucho gusto*, Jake." Pastor Ruiz gave his hand a hearty shake. He turned to look inside the building. "No, I haven't seen them tonight. They both have several kids and come together, so I generally hear them when they arrive. You're welcome to come in and have a seat."

Jake walked inside and scanned the small crowd of people already seated in the rows of chairs. He didn't see any familiar faces. In most rooms in Port Provident, Jake knew everyone and they all knew him. The Peoples family put down roots on this island before Texas became an independent republic, more than a century and a half ago. But here at *La Iglesia de la Luz del Mundo*, he didn't know the neighborhood. He didn't speak the language. He didn't recognize the faces. Jake stood completely alone in the middle of his hometown.

Looking left, then right, Jake didn't see anyone like him. He squirmed. No one looked his way, but he felt a prickly feeling under his collar as though everyone were staring at him. Maybe he should just go. He'd already done what he'd promised for the City Council. Carter didn't even know about this invitation from Juan and Pablo, so he wouldn't care if Jake ducked it. And the men in question didn't even know he'd come, so it wouldn't look rude if he left.

Jake slid behind the back row of chairs and walked around the perimeter of the room to a small door on the left side of the sanctuary that looked like a good, stealthy escape route. The door did not lead outside, as he'd hoped, but instead to a small hallway, lit with yellowed fluorescent light overhead.

"What are you doing back here?" A woman snapped as she walked down the hall toward him. Jake knew the face, but not the voice. It sounded a shade lower than it should have, and the hair framing the woman's face was six inches too short. "Can't you just leave Gracie in peace? Do you have to ruin church for her, too?"

"Obviously you know who I am, but I don't believe I've met you." Suddenly the walls around him felt more like a cage, trapping him with a fierce tiger.

"Gloria Garcia Rodriguez. Gracie's older sister."

Well, that explained everything. "I'm not here to ruin anything for Gracie. In fact, I'm trying to leave."

"You're not anywhere near an exit. Shame on you, sneaking around the church, trying to dig up dirt to use against Gracie." One finger waggled scoldingly at Jake. "You're wasting your time. This congregation isn't like your high-and-mighty friends. We don't sell out for the highest dollar. We take care of our own, Mr. Peoples."

In the time-honored battle tradition of advancing across the field to confront the enemy, Gloria took a measured step closer to Jake. Facial features weren't the only similarities between the two sisters.

"Is feistiness some kind of family trait?"

"What?" Gloria looked askance.

"Never mind." Jake shook his head. He'd now received the riot act from two Garcia women this week. He just hoped their mother wasn't waiting at the exit, because he couldn't take much more of this.

"Show me the door and I'll get out of your way."

"You'll have to go out through the main sanctuary. Come with me." Gloria pushed past him, bumping his arm.

Jake trailed her down the corridor. Gloria opened the sanctuary door. The seated congregation filled the room, and Pastor Ruiz stood behind the cross-shaped pulpit. If he walked quietly, Jake felt certain he could still make a getaway.

"Gloria—you've found our visitor." The pastor pointed to Jake and his guide. "I'd like everyone to meet Jake Peoples, a friend of the Calderon and Morales families. Please make him feel welcome after the service."

Every head turned to the back of the room. Every pair of eyes fixed on Jake. Including the one pair of chocolate-brown eyes that had filled Jake's thoughts all afternoon.

Gloria stopped and pointed at the seat next to Gracie. "Sit there," she whispered.

It felt strange to be ordered around, but he couldn't see a way out without making a bigger scene. If he left now, it would embarrass two loyal employees.

Jake would not become the kind of boss his father had been, even if it cost him a little pride tonight.

Gracie picked up her purse and a slim copy of the Bible from the chair, then laid them carefully on the floor. Her gaze never wavered from the pastor at the pulpit.

As in most Texas rooms during the summer, the air-conditioning couldn't quite overpower the lingering heat inside the church. Jake couldn't feel the stuffiness, though. Gracie's cold shoulder gave him a chill.

"Tonight, *amigos*, I want to share with you Jesus's own words from the book of Matthew." The pastor opened his Bible and adjusted the microphone attached to the top of the lectern. "Last week, we talked about the first part of Jesus's reply when he was asked about the greatest commandment. First, He told us to love God with everything we have. In the second part of the answer, he says to 'love your neighbor as yourself.'"

Jake had heard this one before. Now, stuck uncomfortably next to Gracie, he was going to have to sit through the same old stuff he'd been listening to since he first saw Jesus's life played out on a flannelboard in childhood Sunday school. Different building, same message. The only difference—the unfamiliar faces. Everything else about churches was the same—old, boring. Jake looked down at the floor. A lifetime of sitting in the Peoples family pew at First Provident Church had taught him how to zone out just enough to make it through an hour of church. Of course, he never had to do so with Gracie Garcia sitting about ten inches from him.

"I want to challenge all of us tonight to think about this verse in a new way. Who are our neighbors? Just the people who live in our neighborhood? Just the friends we see at school or at work?" The pastor paused a moment, letting the words sink in. "No, *amigos*. Jesus is calling us to expand our horizons. We all have someone in our lives we need to see from a fresh perspective, someone whose shoes we need to walk in. Who is that person in your life?"

Paying half attention to the words being preached, Jake's mind wandered.

"Getting real with people requires getting out of our comfort zone," Pastor Ruiz said. "But we must remember, *amigos*, the most important things in life are not things."

Hearing some variant of that phrase for the third time in a matter of days hooked Jake's attention. Focusing on the man at the front of the room, Jake found that he suddenly wanted to pay attention. Crazy, since he couldn't remember a time in church when he'd not obsessively checked his watch.

As Pastor Ruiz began to summarize the evening's lesson, a rustle to his right broke Jake's concentration. Gracie shifted in her seat, uncrossing, then recrossing her legs. Jake noticed her pointy little black shoes.

The pastor invited the congregation to close in prayer. Jake closed his eyes, but Gracie's feet stayed in his mind.

"Amen," Pastor Ruiz concluded. "*Vaya con Dios este semana, amigos*."

Go with God this week, friends. It was a good thing Jake had spent much of his youth on construction sites, where he'd picked up some basic Spanish.

"Excuse me." Gracie stood up, trying to exit the row. Her words revealed none of the fire and determination from the incident outside the sales office. Jake stood and stepped out into the aisle so she could pass. The little black leather heels tapped as she walked by without saying anything more.

He didn't understand Gracie's hot-and-cold attitude. One minute, she seemed fired up. The next, she acted quiet as a mouse. In the condo office parking lot, she drew a line in the sand and promised to teach him a lesson. And now? Her little feet couldn't retreat fast enough.

Once again, Jake knew his initial impression of Gracie had to be correct. She just wasn't cut out for the tough world of running a business. Like her shoes, Gracie Garcia looked nice, but lacked substance. Jake looked at his own leather-soled wingtips, then sneaked one more glance at Gracie's black heels walking out the door of the sanctuary. He could never walk in such silly little things. He was thankful "walking in someone's shoes" was, after all, nothing more than a clichéd phrase.

SHE WOULD TRADE ANYTHING to get away from Jake Peoples.

"Why, Gloria? Why did he actually come tonight?" Gracie grabbed her older sister by the arm as she fled the sanctuary ahead of Jake. "Isn't it enough that he wants to demolish my home and my business? How do I get away from him?"

"I don't know, *hermana*." Gloria put her arm around Gracie's shoulder as they walked through the parking lot. "We live on an island. You wouldn't get too far."

Setting her Bible, notebook, and a praise and worship CD on the front of the car, she turned to face her sister. "I don't really want to run away from my problems, Gloria, but I don't know how to handle him. He makes me so nervous. I couldn't even listen to Pastor Ruiz tonight. I just kept thinking about what Jake must have thought. I'll bet he goes to First Provident. We don't have stained glass here. We don't have a big fancy pipe organ. He probably sat there the whole time, looking down his nose at us."

"Probably so." Gloria nodded. "And now he's looking across the parking lot at you."

Gracie's stomach flipped like a tortilla on a griddle. "Well, that's all he's going to be able to do. I am not prepared to talk to him tonight. I'm getting in my car and heading home. He can call me tomorrow if he wants to spread more doom and gloom about my future."

"Okay. I'm going to have dinner in the Fellowship Hall. I'll call you later tonight." Gloria waved as she walked off with a group of other churchgoers.

Gracie unlocked the door to her little blue Ford and climbed in. When she slid the key in the ignition and turned it, the car rumbled, gave three chugs, then went silent. She tried it again. Same noises, same silence. Then someone tapped the driver's-side window.

Oh, no.

Her eyes began to roll back in her head and her lungs filled with an instinctive deep breath. Why did he always have to be around to witness her humiliating moments? First almost throwing up in the classroom, now car trouble. She could add impeccable timing to the growing list of reasons why she didn't like the sandy blond-haired businessman.

"Need some help?" Jake's words sounded muffled through the glass.

No, she wanted to say. She'd invited him into her life once, to show him *El Centro por las Lenguas*, and that night became a total mess. She would not make the same mistake two days in a row.

Jake Peoples reminded her of an expression her parents used—*un viento malo*. A bad wind. Living on an island as long as she had, Gracie had seen plenty of squalls. One moment, everything seemed calm, but in the next minute, everything got blown every which way.

Jake's very presence messed with her emotions. One minute she trusted that she could take on the establishment, the next minute, everything came crashing down. In just two days, this battle with Jake had already turned her into a person she didn't care for. But as much as she didn't like fighting with Jake, fighting her car generally turned her into a dirty, greasy mess—something else she didn't particularly like.

Opening the door with great reluctance, Gracie said, "The car's been acting up lately. I think it might be the battery."

"Pop the hood and let me take a look. If it's the battery, I have some jumper cables in the back of my truck." She pulled the black latch inside the car.

Jake raised the heavy Detroit steel, then propped it up. "Do you have a flashlight?" The sun started to slip lower in the sky, and while it wasn't yet dark, the vertical hood blocked the remaining light from reaching the engine area.

"In my trunk. Hold on." Gracie walked around and opened the back of the car, pausing briefly. She felt safe behind the trunk, shielded from Jake. Pulling the flashlight out of the canvas emergency bag she always carried, she steadied herself then carefully stepped back toward Jake.

Tinkering with the battery, the executive looked completely out of place, still dressed in his office attire. This neighborhood was known more for blue jeans and blue collars. Jake's crested, collared knit shirt and starched trousers stood out. Absently, he reached his hand down and wiped it on the twill. A greasy streak stood out clearly just above the knee.

"Oh, no, Jake. Your pants."

He looked down and shrugged. "Typical. I get so lost in a project that I forget to keep track of what's going on around me. Don't worry about it. That's what dry cleaners are for." Jake reached for the flashlight, then shone it around the top of the battery. "Yep, there's your problem. See that ring?"

Gracie craned her neck around the edge of the hood and looked at the clamp on one pole of the battery. She nodded. "It's supposed to be on tight to give a good connection, but for some reason, your screw is rusted out and now it's loose. All the salt air down here is hard on car parts. You'll need a new screw."

"Can I make it home?"

"Afraid not. Your battery isn't making the connection. It's a pretty easy fix, though. I'm sure I've got a part at my place that will work."

"Oh, well...that's okay. I'm sure someone will be out soon who can take me home."

Gracie did not want to owe Jake Peoples anything. Not even one measly piece of metal.

"Gracie, everyone just sat down to dinner. Port Provident isn't that big—I live about ten minutes from here." He pointed east, in the direction of the island's largest collection of historic homes. "We can have your car fixed before everyone finishes eating. There's no sense in interrupting everyone's dinner or making you wait any longer."

His tone didn't surprise Gracie. She'd heard it before. The businessman with all the answers. Unfortunately, she couldn't argue with him. Unlike his insistence on closing her school, this time, his plan made sense. If he could fix the problem quickly, there wasn't any need to disrupt her family and friends while they ate.

The issue of being beholden to Jake, though, felt like an itch in an unreachable place. It bothered her. But there wasn't really anything she could do about it right now.

"Okay. Thanks for the offer." One little round half inch of metal couldn't cost that much in obligation, anyway. She picked up her things off the front seat of the car and followed him down the sidewalk.

Jake jogged in front of Gracie, reaching out to open the passenger door. His small act of chivalry surprised her. Except for her father, she couldn't remember a man opening a car door for her.

"Okay, we should have you fixed up in no time." Jake angled the steering wheel ever-so-slightly to the left, pulling onto the street.

"Thanks again. You really didn't have to do this." "Gracie, my nana would never forgive me if I'd left a lady stranded in a parking lot with a broken-down car." He flashed a quick grin.

"Your nana?" She knew Jake led a family business, but for some silly reason never thought of him as having a family.

"My father's mother. Her favorite author is Emily Post."

Gracie laughed. "I love to read, but even I wouldn't take an etiquette book down to the beach."

"Nana would. And when she'd finished refreshing her memory on proper knife and fork placement, she'd take out monogrammed notecards and a fountain pen to catch up on correspondence."

"She sounds very proper."

"Oh, yes. Her family's been a fixture here in Port Provident since before the Great Storm of 1910." Jake guided the car onto Gulfview Boulevard. "But most people love her because she has a heart as vast as that water over there."

"Sounds like she'd be a good grandmother. I miss my *abuela*."

"That's Spanish for 'grandmother,' right?"

Gracie nodded. "It is."

"So, where is your grandmother?"

"In Mexico. She doesn't like to travel, so we have to go see her. And it's always been hard for my parents to get time off from running their restaurant."

"I know how that feels. I didn't see Nana much during my years in Austin." His eyes fixed on the red light ahead. "Of course, most of that was my own doing."

His last words trailed off and he changed the subject. "Look at the clouds over the water. The sky looks like it's on fire." The setting sun turned the clouds a faint purple, set off by a backdrop of flaming orange.

"God paints a pretty picture, doesn't He?" Gracie joined in the admiration.

Jake didn't answer. Silence fell between them, like a thousand down feathers filling all the spaces in the small cabin of the car. First it tickled gently, fluffily, but then the sharper edges reached out and poked her, making the presence of the quiet too obvious for comfort. Gracie rubbed the cotton folds of her skirt together, then hesitated, not wanting to squirm too obviously.

"Do you have to be anywhere right now?" Jake asked.

"Well, I thought we were going to your house to get the part." *Wasn't he going to help her with the car repair?*

"We still are." His blade-sharp tone cut through her questioning mind. "Do you have time to take a walk on the beach?"

In the short time since Jake had walked into Gracie's life, she'd seen many sides of him. Authoritative. Impatient. Driven. Never impulsive.

Without waiting for her answer, he pulled the car into a parking spot close to the water's edge, demonstrating a trait Gracie did recognize: decisiveness.

She couldn't figure this out. "Why, Jake?"

He shut off the ignition, then rested his fingers on the door handle. "You said it yourself, Gracie. God painted a pretty picture tonight on the horizon. And Pastor Ruiz talked about walking earlier."

"He used a metaphor. I don't think he really meant for you to take up a new fitness routine."

Jake opened the door and stepped out quickly to avoid the passing traffic on Gulfview Boulevard. He came around to

Gracie's door and reached his hand inside, beckoning her to join him. "I'm not, Gracie. Something the pastor said spoke to me tonight, and I wanted to take his advice."

His hand lingered inside the car, waiting for Gracie's action. Just over Jake's shoulder, she could see a seagull cruising effortlessly on the breeze. Did the seagulls question why they soared? Or did they just trust that the wind would carry them? Could she trust Jake's invitation? Or was it just another calculated move in their game of real estate chess?

The words in her mind muddled together instead of forming a quick prayer as she'd wanted. She could only hope God knew what lay in her heart at this moment. And then, as she felt the breeze dance through her hair, an answer came in the form of another carefree bird riding above the waves in front of her. Like the seagull, she needed to trust.

She lifted her hand and laid it cautiously in Jake's palm. He squeezed and tugged back, helping pull her out of the car. His fingertips felt warm as they brushed the center of her wrist, causing the blood in her veins to tingle with awareness. Tonight, she and Jake weren't at her school or her church. She couldn't bolster her confidence with familiar surroundings or faces. A hermit crab without a shell could not have felt any more defenseless.

They walked down a few concrete stairs, then stepped onto the unstable surface of the beach. Her feet pushed small dents in the sand.

"You said you liked something Pastor Ruiz talked about?" She needed to know why Jake had changed their plans. She needed to wrap reason and order around her shoulders.

Standing without her light sweater made Gracie cold in spite of the early summer evening.

"He made me realize I didn't handle myself professionally last night." They walked along the edge of the shoreline, where the waves languidly pulled to a stop just inches from their toes. "I won't lie, Gracie. This condo project has to get done. A lot rides on it. But I came to your school last night with no intention of getting anywhere near your shoes, much less walking in them."

"But if you still say the condo project has to get done your way, why do you care about my shoes tonight? Nothing's changed, Jake."

"I don't know, Gracie. I do know you care about your students. I know they care about you." He stopped and faced her. "But I run a company whose board of directors will not confirm me as CEO if I can't pull this deal off. I suppose I just want you to know it's not personal."

She'd never looked squarely into his eyes before. They were a shade of green she hadn't seen since leaving Mexico's Yucatán coast as a child. "Maybe it's not personal to you, but it is to me. You want to demolish my home and my business for a swimming pool. You're trying to sink my life's mission."

The salt in the air smelled like tears. Even the sky reflected how hopeless Gracie felt about the situation.

"Surely you can move the business somewhere else, Gracie."

"Jake, I can't. The economy might be tough in other places, but this is a resort town. The price of real estate hasn't declined. I can't afford to rent another building and an apartment on top of that. I'm a one-woman show. The connection fees and deposits alone for a new location would wipe out what little savings I have." Admitting her precarious financial situation cost her a big chunk of pride. "You come from a wealthy family. You've never struggled to pay the bills."

He gave a short laugh. Gracie felt more pride tear away, like a bandage ripping off delicate skin. She hadn't expected to hear him dismiss her in return for her honesty. She turned her head toward the surf. If a tear slipped out, she couldn't let Jake see.

"Gracie, look here." He placed a gentle finger on her chin and pressed her to look at him straight on. The touch sent her blood rushing through her veins again. "I'm laughing at the irony. You and I have more in common than you realize. I told you the board of directors doesn't want me in charge of my own family's company, but I didn't tell you why. My whole life, my father told anyone who would listen that I wasn't living up to the family name. I spent the last five years in Austin as an attorney with my own firm. I misjudged a client. I put everything I had into her case. In the end, the only courtroom I saw was personal bankruptcy court, which confirmed every ugly word my father ever used against me."

His hands brushed the top of her arms, reminding her of earlier in the school parking lot when he'd rejected her mentorship idea. "Gracie, I've missed paying so many bills, there are judgments against me. And no company wants a bankrupt dreamer as a CEO. I have to prove to the board that there's more to me than the rumors they've heard."

Surely the roaring of the waves had distorted Jake's words. He had to be the spoiled rich kid she'd assumed he was. She couldn't fathom a member of the Peoples family in a situation as desperate as her own.

The color in Jake's eyes deepened. Simultaneously, with a single step, he closed the distance between them. As the wind kicked a small gust up around them, Gracie didn't take a step back. She could feel something inside her being carried like foam rising at the top of a wave. One arm rose tentatively on a crest of emotion to gently rest on Jake's shoulder. Her fingers fluttered through the soft strands of hair covering the upper part of his neck. She knew what shouldn't happen next but, like the waves behind her, didn't know how to stop it. Jake's green eyes connected boldly with her own, looking for something.

And then he moved his feet back to where they'd stood moments before. Gracie slid her arm away. The waves in the distance continued their swells and rolls as Gracie's emotions came crashing back to the sand.

She felt betrayed by her own impulsiveness. She couldn't believe she was making the same mistakes again—thinking with her heart, not with her head. Hadn't she learned anything from her time with David? She had to remember that the same Jake Peoples who had mesmerized her just moments ago could steal her dreams and her future with just one vote from his friends on City Council. She could not allow him to steal her heart.

Chapter Five

JAKE TRIED TO USE THE soft sand beneath his feet to explain feeling off balance. It couldn't be that walking near Gracie Garcia rocked his world. Jake couldn't let the moment pass without saying something. But what? What sense could he make of the unexpected, wordless moment that clearly lay on them both with an undeniable weight? He couldn't just ignore it, much as he wanted to play it cool.

Before he could match words with his racing emotions, Gracie spoke. "We should probably go. My car needs to be fixed before everyone comes out and sees me with you. People are beginning to ask questions about the closing of the school, and after you showed up tonight..." She paused, looking out at the waves. "Well, I just don't want to have to answer everyone's questions."

Like a surfboard standing in the sand, a wall went up between the two of them. He immediately sensed the barrier's instant appearance. Many dates in Jake's youth ended on this very stretch of beach. Most of them finished with a kiss. But all that sloppy teenage ardor couldn't compare to the surge of adrenaline that filled him when Gracie stood near.

In the past, he could always tell when the feelings were mutual. Now, though, Jake couldn't read Gracie. He knew he hadn't imagined her arms around his neck. He couldn't possibly have made up the tingle at the top of his spine when she threaded her narrow fingers through his hair.

Maybe he'd just made more out of the events because he hadn't been here in so long. Maybe he really wasn't the family businessman who could accurately assess a situation and react accordingly. Maybe he remained the lawyer from Austin who got caught up in what he wanted to see instead of what was actually there. Without a word, he turned toward the car.

The corner lot holding the Victorian house in which Jake's grandmother lived sprawled across half a city block. As they pulled through the back gate near the refurbished carriage house Jake rented from Nana, he noticed Gracie's head turn slightly. Was she wondering how many of the modest homes from the neighborhood surrounding Gracie's church would fit within Nana's ornate wrought-iron fence? Jake had never thought about Nana's estate in those terms before, but now he couldn't help it.

Gracie didn't let out so much as one syllable to help Jake understand her thoughts. In fact, she hadn't uttered a single word since she asked Jake to leave the beach. Thankfully, the drive didn't last long. Each passing minute stuffed more awkward silence into the car, pressing around them until he noticed that there remained very little room to even breathe.

"I'll be right back." He couldn't get out of the car fast enough, but then slowed his gait in order to give himself the maximum amount of time away from the uncomfortable silence. The workshop adjacent to the garage opened with the same key that had been under the mat for years.

Jake went straight to the upright toolbox in the back corner and pulled out a narrow red drawer on the third row, then rummaged through a small plastic box. Pulling the rusted screw out of his pocket, Jake compared it to a new one to make sure it matched. Satisfied, he pushed the drawer back in, walked over to the door and locked up.

The whole trip to the workshop couldn't have lasted more than two minutes. Jake wished it could have eaten more time off the clock. In fact, he wished he could have turned the clock all the way back to their earlier drive down Gulfview Boulevard, before he decided to take the detour to the beach.

That's what he got for listening to all that church nonsense. Feeling moved to walk in Gracie's shoes had gotten him nothing but the verbal equivalent of a blister. God probably thought it was funny that Jake got Pastor Ruiz's message so wrong.

Jake would not give God, Gracie Garcia or anyone else the ammunition to point out his mistakes again. No more church, no more benefits of the doubt. Only a few days remained until he would prove he could be the CEO Peoples Property Group needed. No mistakes from his time in Austin, no more mistakes in his time with Gracie. No more mistakes period.

His future depended on leading Peoples Property Group. Not on a teacher in Port Provident today—or one from Jerusalem two thousand years ago.

Tossing and turning all night left Gracie's back sore and her head with a dull pain just over her right temple.

She'd never before experienced a non-kiss that made her lose sleep.

She'd never before dreamed about a man who wanted to steal her life's dreams.

She lost track of the number of times she'd awakened last night. Nothing helped. Not even counting sheep. All she'd wanted to count was the number of beats her heart skipped when Jake's hands had brushed her arms. Even now, hours after waking, every time her thoughts wandered to last night's walk on the beach, Gracie lost the battle. But this month's budget and bill paying called and conquering the pile of papers covering the left side of her desk would take focus, not flights of fancy.

Gracie pulled out a pen and a book of stamps and set them alongside her computer keyboard, then opened her small business accounting software. Before she could start, she heard a knock at the office door.

"Come in," Gracie said, distracted once again from the task at hand.

"*Holá, hermana*!" Gloria's voice blew a beam of sunshine into the room. "It's a beautiful day outside. Why are you sitting in the middle of a sea of paperwork? You should be dipping your toes in the water instead."

Dressed in a floppy turquoise straw hat, a light cotton blouse and shorts, and a pair of matching rhinestone-bedecked flip-flops, Gloria looked ready for the beach.

"Because I didn't build my business by slacking off. I may only be treading water right now, but if I stop, everything I've worked for will drown."

"Gracie, don't you think you're being overly dramatic?"

If her sister only knew about that turn of events at the beach last night. "No, Gloria, I don't. Jake told me he has to complete this stupid condo project in order to get the company's board of directors to confirm him as the permanent

CEO. If he doesn't shut my school down ASAP, he'll lose his job. Do you really think he's going to let that happen?"

Gloria shook her head. "No, I guess not. When did he tell you this?"

"Last night after church." Gracie pulled another bill out of the stack.

"I thought you said you weren't going to talk to him."

"I wasn't. Then my car wouldn't start. He helped me out."

"I see." Gloria slowly leaned back against the door to the office. Gracie could tell her sister picked up on something unspoken. "So he told you his life story while he jumped your battery?"

Oh, he'd given her a charge last night, for sure. But Gloria didn't need to know about that. "Well, no. We had to go to his nana's house to pick up a part for the car."

"He took you to his grandmother's house?" Gloria crossed her arms. Gracie started to feel as though she sat on the stand, not behind her desk. "I stayed in the car while he got the part from her garage," she answered.

"So, when did he tell you about his job? I know where the Peoples estate is. It's not far from the church. You'd barely have time to have a good conversation."

Gloria's ability to sniff out details kept her midwifery patients healthy and safe during pregnancy and labor. At present, though, it pushed her younger sister into the danger zone. Long ago, Gracie and Gloria promised not to keep secrets from each other. She couldn't break that promise, even now. But would she really have to tell everything? She could still be truthful and not...well...almost-kiss-and-tell, right?

"You're tapping your pen, Gracie. What are you hiding?"

"Nothing, really. We stopped at the beach for a few minutes while we were on the way to his house." She pulled a bill out of the stack and started to write a check. If she was using the pen, she couldn't very well tap it and tip off the sibling investigation squad any further. Besides, by watching what she was doing, she didn't have to look at Gloria.

"*Mm-hmm*. So, on your way to fix your broken-down car, you stop at the beach, where your business rival tells you he has to shut down your school or lose his job." Gloria walked across the room as she spoke, coming to stand just across the desk from her sister.

Gracie gripped the pen tightly and reached for another bill. "More or less."

The phone began to ring, cutting off Gracie's fight not to incriminate herself any further. After a quick glance at the caller ID, however, she decided not to answer.

"Aren't you going to get that?" Gloria asked.

"No." The only person she wanted to say less to than Gloria was on the other end of the line. Gloria stretched to read the caller ID screen, then with one quick motion, punched the speakerphone button. "Hello."

"Hey, it's Jake. I'm on my way over to your school. We need to talk. I know that moment on the beach complicated things..."

"Graciela Garcia de Piedra! *Eres loca*? Did you kiss him?" Gloria's outburst probably blasted out the speaker on Jake's cell phone.

"Gloria, I'm not crazy. Now hush." Gracie shot a stern look at her sister and picked up the receiver. She would say as little as possible while in the company of her shocked sibling. "Okay, Jake. I'm just here doing some paperwork."

"Your sister's there? Do you need me to wait?"

"She was just headed to Surfside Beach." Gracie tried to force confidence into her voice, but barely trusted herself around Jake after last night.

"Okay, I'm on Gulfview. I'll see you in about five minutes." She laid the handset softly in the cradle, hoping Gloria would be as gentle with her.

No such luck.

"Graciela, what do you mean that you're not crazy? After church you said you didn't want talk to him—but somehow, a few minutes later, you find yourself on the beach, having a 'moment'? *Explica*, por favor."

"I didn't kiss him. I promise. I don't know how to explain it, Gloria. It just happened."

"Gracie, nothing ever 'just happens' to you. You're the most deliberate planner I know. It drives you crazy to assist me with births because you can't organize labor."

Gloria didn't realize how perfectly her reminder fit the situation. Just as the natural process of childbirth seemed to take over Gloria's clients, being there on the beach last night with Jake felt organic. Gracie could no more have held back from being attracted to Jake than a mother could keep from pushing on a contraction.

"I know, Gloria. We'll talk it through when he gets here. It's not going to happen again." Gracie tapped her pen on the desk in a quick rat-a-tat.

Gloria quirked an eyebrow at the display of nervous energy. "Sure it won't."

"I'm serious, Gloria. I know now he doesn't have any help to offer me, regardless of what the City Council expects. I'm just going to tell him I understand that and I'll find a solution on my own. I should hear about that grant any day, and once I get that funding, it'll be tough, but I'll rearrange some priorities and do what it takes to keep the school running...somewhere, somehow." Gracie looked straight at her sister, making a promise with her eyes. "I'm going to meet with him right now and explain it, then I won't need to see him again until the City Council meeting, when I'll have come up with something by myself."

"*Bien*." Reaching out, Gloria patted Gracie on the hand. "I'll let you take care of business. I'll be at the beach for a little while if you want to join me when you're through."

Gloria turned toward the office door.

"Okay. This shouldn't take long, and then I need to run by my P.O. box to check for that grant letter. I'll call you later and see if you're still down at the beach. A little break with some sand and sun sounds like just what the doctor ordered to take my mind off things."

After Gloria left, Gracie tried to collect her thoughts in the few minutes before Jake's arrival. Last night, he said things between them weren't personal, only business.

Then with no warning, everything turned very personal. Too personal.

These days, Gracie couldn't afford many extras. She knew about prioritizing. And even though she'd thought of nothing else but last night's moment in the moonlight, the price was too high.

Saving El Centro was the only thing that mattered. She needed a plan. She needed new options. She did not need Jake Peoples. She didn't need anything that took her away from running her school and remaining available to her students. Attraction and relationships, even of the casual kind, didn't have a place in her life's budget.

When she'd broken that rule and made time in her life for David, she got shortchanged. She wouldn't let that happen again.

In order to save her school—her life's work—she couldn't.

The bell on the front door jingled, breaking into Gracie's thoughts. The instant Jake walked through the office door, his presence filled the small space. Even though he was dressed casually in khaki pants and a navy knit polo shirt, Gracie's breath caught a little in her throat.

She couldn't take her eyes off him. He looked polished. He looked unaffordable.

"Gracie, I need to apologize to you..."

Jake's words began to flow out with a rush, but Gracie interrupted. "Really, Jake, if we just—"

He cut her words off. Two strides closed the distance between them. "Gracie, you don't need to say anything. This is my fault." He leaned against the desk, using his hand for balance. He came so close to Gracie that she could feel the heat his body generated.

She couldn't help but stare. Five fingers, with neatly trimmed nails. The faintly defined muscles in his arm showed the effort of a man who worked out, but not to excess. Remembering how much she'd let her guard down and wanted those arms to hold her last night made Gracie's eyelids slide closed.

She didn't want Jake to apologize.

"Gracie? You can't even look at me now?" Jake's voice cracked.

"No, Jake. That's not it at all. It's just...just my head." Gracie flicked her wrist dismissively.

He looked at the piles of papers scattered across the desktop. "Paying bills usually gives me a headache, too. I know how you feel."

She hoped not. If he truly could read her mind, they'd have an even bigger mess on their hands.

"Thanks," she said softly, unable to think of anything else.

"I have an offer to make to you." Gracie forced herself to look up. His green eyes reminded her of the ink on a dollar bill. The harsh reality remained that she needed more dollars and less Jake.

"What do you mean?" "Remember when I told you last night that Pastor Ruiz's words made me realize I hadn't treated you fairly?"

"Yes." Gracie nodded. She remembered every step and every syllable of that walk on the beach.

"Well, it's true. And I stayed up last night trying to figure out what to do about it."

At least she hadn't been the only one awake all night. "I don't understand, Jake. You told me the condo project had to be built and you needed this land."

"That's correct, Gracie. But I went through our property list last night, looking for a place where you could move."

"But the other day, Mitch Carson said your company had no other place to move me and he wouldn't give me a letter to even take to other potential landlords."

"Mitch doesn't run the company. I do. Something may work out. It may not. But the last CEO of Peoples Property Group didn't always treat people fairly and I do not intend to follow in his footsteps."

For all her earlier determination about making things work, Gracie knew it would take more than a property list. She possessed no savings, and until she checked her post office box, no notification of receiving the grant money.

"Jake, that's nice of you, but nothing about my situation has changed. I need a place for the school and a place to live, and I just don't have the funds to move right now."

Gracie knew of only one solution: a miracle.

"I remembered all that and took it into account. The bad news is that Peoples Property Group doesn't have anything available that meets your needs."

Gracie's heart sank before she'd even realized her hopes had risen at Jake's words. "Is there any good news?"

"Yes. I called my friend Melissa Miller this morning. She's a local real estate agent, and she's pulled a few current listings that might work for you. I thought we could meet her and go look at them."

Jake lifted his hand from the desk and took Gracie's. Her heart skipped a beat from the brush of his palm against hers. Then it skipped another beat at the thought of a possible solution to her problem.

"When?"

"She's available this afternoon. I know we didn't get off to the right start. And then there was that mess at the beach."

Gracie wasn't sure she liked their near-kiss being dismissed as *that mess*. But any kind of relationship with Jake was out of the question. Even though Jake had fallen on some personal tough times, men who grew up in historic estates in Port Provident did not get involved with women who didn't have the money to save their own business. And women who were trying to prevent their life's work from being crushed shouldn't think about the men turning their world upside down anyway. She had to maintain her focus.

For years, singular vision kept El Centro open in spite of precarious finances and other challenges. Gracie scolded herself silently. She couldn't abandon a philosophy that had worked for her for years.

"Are you ready to go?" Jake jingled the keys in his pocket.

The Bible spoke over and over again about the value God placed on hard work. He didn't reward idle hands. She'd done everything within these four walls to keep El Centro open. Maybe God brought Jake here today to show she needed to make a renewed effort, this time outside her comfort zone. Just as Pastor Ruiz had said yesterday. Stay focused, but look for new horizons.

"I think so. These can wait." Gracie pushed the bills aside, then reached below the desk for her purse.

For the first time today, she felt like smiling. Glancing Heavenward, Gracie prayed silently as she locked the front door behind them. *Please God, help me see the plan you have for me and for El Centro. Show me where we need to go.*

Gracie saw the "For Lease" sign in the window of the fourth and final property on the real estate agent's list. The first three locations showed great potential for living and learning, but all seemed far out of her price range—even with the possible grant funding.

But this last building, on the edge of Port Provident's historic downtown district, came with a lower price tag. "As you can see, this location is no-frills." Gracie found herself impressed with Melissa Miller. So far, she'd been straightforward and honest about each place they'd looked, giving Gracie both the positives and the negatives.

The former location of the State Street Title Company didn't boast fancy floors or custom fixtures. In fact, the trio's footsteps echoed with each footfall on plain concrete. Overhead, white rectangular fixtures lined up in rows for simple, functional illumination. But the windows across the front and side of this corner location more than made up for the limited amenities. Natural light flowed across the room, making the featherings of dust in the air dance and sparkle.

"I can see myself teaching in here. The open floor plan would suit a classroom layout well. And that little room in the back corner could work for an office."

The agent nodded agreeably. "I thought you might like this location. And as I mentioned on the drive over here, there's a small efficiency apartment upstairs. The rest of the building has been converted to luxury lofts, but the previous owner kept a small residence for himself. He had a heart attack before he could finish renovating this space downstairs. His family hopes to lease this space and the living quarters together, even though the historic renovations aren't as far along as those done on other properties in this area."

"Can we see the apartment?" Jake asked. He'd remained largely quiet while they'd toured the properties, letting Gracie ask the questions. She hadn't expected his quiet presence to be comforting. He allowed her to be in control, but she knew if she needed his assistance, it would be there.

"Absolutely." Melissa threw a pageant-worthy smile at Jake.

"Gracie, do you want to see anything else downstairs?" Gracie looked around the room one last time and almost breathed a sigh of relief. For the first time in days, it felt like a viable option lay in front of her. Or at least she hoped the option would prove legitimate.

Earlier, Melissa gave Gracie a paper with details about the property, including the monthly rent. Although a slight increase above what Gracie currently paid to Jake's company, with the grant money, she might be able to afford it.

The key word, of course, was *might*. Which rhymed with *tight*. Which Gracie's budget would undoubtedly be if she moved in here.

Gracie tried doing some simple math in her head. She wanted to know if she could make this location a reality before pinning her hopes on it. She paused to think.

"Oof." Jake stumbled into the stationary Gracie. Reaching out to steady himself on the narrow stairs, Jake clutched Gracie's waist. Facts and figures took flight from her head as her heart leapt in her chest. Instinct guided Jake's movements more than anything, but Gracie's own reflexes melted at his touch.

"I'm sorry," she said, not really meaning it. "Don't be. I should have been more careful. I was just admiring the woodwork on this banister. This building survived the Great Storm of 1910. I'm always blown away by the craftsmanship in the historic homes and buildings here in Port Provident."

He slid his palm slowly back and forth across the dark mahogany, almost caressing the grain. Gracie wondered if she could possibly harbor jealousy toward an inanimate object.

In fact, if she didn't know better, she'd think she was developing a crush on Jake, the way these thoughts kept popping up in her mind. She'd do well to remember that crushes never worked out for her.

"I like this building," he said. "If the apartment suits you, it could be a good option."

Gracie nodded in agreement. "I've been trying to add up all the numbers in my head, but math never was my strongest subject. I need a calculator and a notepad."

His hand patted her shoulder blade solidly. "You're in luck. I happen to love math. Maybe we could go to lunch after we're finished here, then go back to your office and see what the numbers say."

If she said yes, she could bask in the light of his green eyes all afternoon. But although he'd brought the torch of reconciliation to her school today, Jake Peoples remained her rival. As of this moment, they both needed the land where *El Centro por las Lenguas* stood.

She appreciated that he now took his promise to her and the City Council seriously. But even though she'd told him more than once she didn't have any money to spare, opening up the spreadsheets and showing him the full precariousness of her financial situation would feel like giving battle plans to the enemy.

"Oh, Jake, I don't know. I think I need to digest all this myself, first." Besides, any number crunching needed to include the amount of grant money, a number she did not yet possess. A number she might never possess.

Gracie pushed the negative thought aside. She needed to stay positive. Plus, a historic apartment about four stairs away awaited her inspection.

"Jake? Are you coming?" Melissa's voice came from inside the apartment.

"Yeah. On our way." Jake gave Gracie a playful shove. "Ready to see your new home?"

"Ready." Gracie nodded. The dance of the butterflies in her stomach slowed at the sight of his white teeth bared in a boyish grin.

She was ready to know where her school would operate after next week.

She was ready to know where she'd live.

She was ready to learn if she received the grant money.

And above all, she was ready to stop wondering what it would be like if she let her guard down once more for an all-American, local native son.

JAKE COULDN'T HELP but notice the light in Gracie's eyes as she looked around the efficiency apartment. The place reminded him a bit of his own snug lodgings in the former carriage house at his grandmother's estate. Not a lot of room, but clean and bright and large enough for her to be comfortable here.

And happy. Seeing Gracie's smile made his own mouth turn up at the corners. Jake's thoughts turned briefly from the intriguing woman in front of him to his father.

See, Old Man, combining some compassion with your career can be done. I can't wait to get into that board meeting tomorrow. I'm going to be able to show them the condo deal is done and I didn't have to hurt anyone in the process. Trust isn't necessarily bad for business.

Now, Jake needed Gracie to reconsider his lunch invitation. Last night on the beach, he told her how he knew she cared about her students and they cared about her. But he carefully guarded the thought that he'd started to see Gracie in a new light. Now that things seemed to be working out for both of them, he could allow himself to admit that Gracie's students weren't the only ones who cared about the feisty teacher with the sun-kissed skin.

Before, he'd pushed those thoughts aside. He had to remember he still needed to pass muster before the Peoples Property Group board. Even with that thought foremost in his mind, Jake couldn't help but notice the other businessperson in the equation.

Gracie didn't take things for granted. She'd come with her family to Port Provident to create a new life. She'd built a business through hard work. And when that business came under threat, she hadn't lied and played games the way the last client he'd worked with in Austin had.

Gracie tackled the challenge head-on. More than that, she'd relied on her faith and been open about it. Jake had never met an entrepreneur who consulted God instead of going to a board of advisors. He'd been raised to believe that churches were nothing more than buildings and showing up on Sundays was nothing more than an appointment on the calendar.

You needed to see and be seen, then move on with the other six days in the week. Jake knew he didn't want to do business in the same cold, calculating manner as his father had. That conviction made him leave Port Provident in the first place, and even though his law practice hadn't worked out, his convictions hadn't changed.

But Gracie's partnership with God challenged Jake's ideas of corporate relationships. Somehow, Jake knew that long after the ink dried on the City Council's resolution and they'd gone their separate ways, Gracie would not disappear from his mind.

"Jake?" Melissa pulled him back into the here and now. "As her current landlord, you'd be able to get a reference pulled together for Gracie, right? Could you do it by this afternoon?"

Jake noticed Gracie's shoulders stiffen at Melissa's question. She remembered Mitch's admonishment the other day. He'd deferred to Mitch then, but knew he now needed to step up and be the leader of Peoples Property Group in both name and in action.

"Sure. I'll call Anne. She or one of our other administrative assistants probably already has a reference letter on file that can be customized for Gracie. I'll have her fax it over to you."

Beyond the effect Melissa's real estate listings had on Gracie, wouldn't Carter Porter and the rest of the City Council be surprised when he showed up with an actual solution? Jake knew he'd pretty much surprised himself by taking this assignment seriously and solving the issue for both parties. Surely revealing this to the board of directors would demonstrate his work ethic. He'd found a solution when the local government only expected a minimal effort.

But could he explain to his hard-nosed board of directors that he had the pastor of a church to thank for the inspiration behind the plan?

"Gracie, you're smiling. Do you like this location?" The sight made Jake even more glad he'd called Melissa.

"I do, Jake." She walked to the front window and looked out across downtown. "Thank you. I hope I can make this work."

"Great." The real estate agent picked up a black leather portfolio off the table and began to write down a few notes. "I'll be waiting for the go-ahead call from you, Gracie, and the reference letter from you, Jake. We can present the offer this afternoon."

The three of them headed back downstairs. Gracie stopped a few steps down the sidewalk and looked back at the building. A gulf breeze caused the wide ruffle of her long, white sundress to flutter around her ankles. The sun's rays brushed across Gracie's shoulders, causing her cappuccino complexion to take on a golden glow. Another small puff of wind picked up the ends of her thick ponytail, then dropped it down in a casual tousle.

Jake couldn't turn away.

"Gracie? You sure I can't take you to lunch? We're less than a block from the Starfish Grill." He couldn't stand to let the afternoon end.

"I really should get back and start plugging in those numbers, Jake. I'd like to have an answer for Melissa today. Plus, I still need to go to the post office and check my mail."

Her dark eyes met his and dropped kindling on the fire inside him. "You can't think on an empty stomach. I'll even pick up the tab. And then, we'll swing by the post office on our way back to your school."

"I don't know, Jake." Gracie's gaze began to dart around in a distracted manner.

"Yes, you do. Don't look for a reason to say no. I've made you an offer you can't refuse." Jake unlocked the truck. "Take the cannoli."

"Take the what?" Her head tilted, one eyebrow raised skyward, the other crinkled inward toward her nose. Confusion was spelled out gently across every inch of her face.

"Cannoli. It's a line from The Godfather. I said I'd made you an offer you couldn't refuse..." Jake trailed off, seeing she still didn't know what he alluded to. "It's a movie."

"I haven't seen a whole lot of movies. When I was younger, my parents were pretty strict about what Gloria and I could watch. And now that I'm older, I just don't have the time."

"But do you have the time to go to lunch with me?" He opened the passenger-side door with a small flourish.

She raised her hands halfway, in an abbreviated gesture of surrender. "You drive a hard bargain, Jake."

"Always." Maybe he did have some of his old man in him after all.

Jake's weekly dinners with Nana almost always took place at the Starfish Grill. He knew what he wanted to eat before he even walked through the door. Gracie, however, took her time. She opened the menu, closed it to read the specials on the back, then opened the folder again without ever saying a word.

"Want me to recommend something?" Jake offered.

"That would be great. I've never been here before, although its reputation precedes it." She looked over the top of the menu.

Her warm, brown eyes stoked a reminder of his favorite item on the dessert tray, molten chocolate cake.

"Do you prefer seafood, or an entrée like chicken?"

"I like seafood. I'm always pushing Mamí and Papí to add more daily specials with local catches at their place, Huarache's."

"Then you'll love the snapper à la Starfish. It's red snapper, caught right out there in the Gulf of Mexico, grilled to perfection and topped with a cream sauce containing shrimp, scallops and asparagus."

"Sounds rich." She closed the menu and laid it gently on the table. "Decision made."

"You won't regret it. I usually tell myself to try something different, but then I remember how heavenly the snapper is. My order never changes."

The waitress came and brought the Caesar salads they'd decided on as an appetizer, then took the order for two snappers à la Starfish. Jake watched Gracie from across the table. Her posture seemed more relaxed than he'd ever seen it, including during their walk on the beach.

"I want to thank you for setting up the showings with Melissa, Jake." She speared a piece of romaine lettuce. "That went above and beyond what I could have expected from this whole mess."

Jake gave complete honesty in return for her compliment. "Look, Gracie, I didn't give much thought to how presenting that eviction notice would affect you. But in the meantime, I was forced to think about it. But I don't want to make you uncomfortable right now by talking about the eviction paper. Let's just enjoy lunch as friends."

"Thank you. Your big meeting is tomorrow, right?" She took the opportunity to change the subject.

"Yes. I'll be presenting my work on the Provident Plaza Condominiums to the board of directors of the Peoples Property Group as an interview of sorts. I've been the interim CEO for a little while now, but I need their approval to make the position official. It's more or less a formality. The company is run by the family, but the board has to give their thumbs-up. In my case, though, there's a lot of bad history between my father and me that needs to be overcome. Sometimes I'm afraid the board will dig up some second cousin of mine and say they'd rather have him as CEO than me because he comes with less baggage."

The waitress brought their entrées and set them carefully on the table. The smell of garlic and spices combined with the sweet aroma of pan-fried snapper almost made Jake lose his train of thought.

"This looks wonderful, Jake. I can't wait to taste it." Gracie pushed her fork into the fish and swirled the bite around in the sauce. "I remember you said you'd been living in Austin. What brought you back to Port Provident? The job?"

"After my dad died, Nana asked me to come home. My law practice in Austin had folded and, as I told you, I'd filed for bankruptcy because of it. I needed a job to pay off my settlement. I didn't have any good reasons to tell her no."

"Your family's company has been around for a long time. I guess you always knew you'd run it someday, right?"

"That's a logical assumption, but no." Jake assembled a final bite of the succulent snapper as he talked. "My father and I didn't get along. I went to law school just so I wouldn't have to work for the company. He didn't care who he stepped on, as long as he got his way. After eighteen years of growing up with that, I left for college and never looked back."

The years peeled away as he spoke. In his mind, Jake saw every detail of that last showdown with his father before leaving for the University of Texas. "In my heart, I always wondered how we could be related. I've never been able to treat anyone—especially family—the way my father treated his only son. I don't have that innate ruthless distrust. Anyway, there came a point when I wanted to remove myself from his presence and stop the doubts in my head about why we never got along. I needed a change of scenery to do that."

"So that's why tomorrow is so important to you? You need to prove your father and those who listened to him wrong." Gracie laid her knife and fork carefully at the top of the plate. "I understand the need to prove doubters wrong."

She reached her hand across the table, then covered Jake's own and gave it a quick pat. The spontaneous gesture of solidarity surprised him.

"I once had someone in my life who said I was important to him," she said. "Then, little by little, David started to treat me as though who I was, where I came from and the people who made up my friends and family weren't good enough for him. He thought I should have been grateful to him to become a part of his world and leave my own behind. It took a while, but I had to learn to stand up for myself and the things that made me the person I am."

Jake almost couldn't believe Gracie's story. What kind of man could tell a woman he cared about her, but she'd have to change in order to keep his affections? The cruelty inherent in that made Jake think back to a different relationship in his own life—the one with his father. He never knew exactly why his father treated him coldly, but from his earliest memories, he knew he didn't measure up.

Jake knew what it felt like to be rejected for who you were, and the knowledge that someone would try to crush Gracie's fiery spirit and the dreams that her family and culture had shaped infuriated him. Jake had brought Gracie to see new properties today as an olive branch, an opportunity to do the right thing. But now, he wanted more. He wanted to protect Gracie from people who didn't show her the proper respect—a mistake he'd made when he first showed up on her doorstep.

Frustrated, he pushed back from the table, the shove to the chair having to substitute for the shove he'd like to give this David character. Learning this new facet of Gracie's past made Jake see just why she wasn't backing down in the present. Jake had once doubted Gracie and her motivations. Not anymore. Tomorrow, he hoped the board of directors of Peoples Property Group would say the same about him.

Chapter Six

GRACIE SHUFFLED THROUGH the collection of envelopes in her post office box. She saw letters from relatives in Mexico, a few bills, and some other correspondence—but not the one item she really hoped for. Another pound of weight settled on Gracie's shoulders with each step she took back to the truck.

"So?" Jake's good-natured inquiry came as soon as Gracie opened the door.

"The letter still hasn't come." She held onto the door handle and boosted herself inside. "I can't move forward with leasing that new place until I know if I've been awarded the grant. Without it, I'm back at square one. I hate this." She would give anything to lose this heaviness and stand up straight again.

Jake pushed a button on the dashboard, silencing the stereo system. "What do you mean?"

"At the beginning of the week, I was the proud owner of a small business that both made ends meet— albeit tightly—and made a difference. Now, all I can think about is how I don't have enough money to continue my work." She placed her elbow on the edge of the door and rested her chin in the cup of her hand, looking blankly at the ocean as they turned onto Gulfview Boulevard. "I never used to think about money all the time. I used to believe that, like the lilies of the field, God would provide everything I needed."

Jake steered the car into a U-turn. "What's changed, Gracie?"

"What do you mean?" Jake's sudden deviation from the route back to her school made Gracie's sense of control fall even more.

"I mean, why can't you trust anymore?" He continued west on Gulfview, toward the end of the island. "It seems to me that not much has changed. You were pinning your hopes on that grant check long before my company's condo project ever entered the picture."

The reality of Jake's words hit Gracie with full force, buffeting her with the impact of his truth.

"Gracie, when I was in Austin watching my career and my law practice go through the shredder, I thought I couldn't stop moving. I was afraid that if I quit pushing forward, I'd lose my momentum and it would all crumble. It all fell apart anyway, and when the last card came down, the exhaustion of not taking the time for myself consumed me."

Jake pulled the car into the entrance to Surfside Beach. "You said your sister was here at the beach. I'm taking you for a break."

Gracie began to protest, then stopped herself. Maybe Jake had the right idea. Maybe she needed a few minutes to refresh. "Thank you, Jake," she said simply. "Which one is your sister's car?" Jake pointed at the front edge of the sand-covered parking lot.

"Umm...that one." Gracie scanned the rows of cars. "The red Chevy SUV in the far corner."

Jake gave the truck some gas, pushing it across the top of a patch of powdery sand. The maneuver marked Jake as an experienced beach driver. Going any slower on the soft surface would have been a sure way to get the heavy vehicle stuck.

"Here you go." He pulled up behind Gloria's car, applied the brake and unbuckled his seat belt. "Do you see her out there?"

"Actually, I do. That purple umbrella near the shore is hers." Gracie looked forward to seeing no-nonsense Gloria, who always knew just what to say when her little sister needed words of wisdom.

At the same time, Gracie felt reluctant to leave Jake's presence. He'd proven to be so much different than her original assessment. He wasn't a heartless privileged son. Jake Peoples was a man who wanted to do the right thing.

He wanted to take over his family's company so he could set the record straight about his own life and to ensure that the business was run fairly. He believed in people, even sometimes to his own detriment. And he would go the extra mile to do the right thing. They came from different worlds, but she and Jake had a lot in common.

The realization made Gracie smile.

"You look really pretty when you do that, you know."

"Do what?"

"Smile. It lights up your face. You're a beautiful woman, Gracie. Especially when you forget to be worried."

"Oh, Jake, I don't know about that."

"You shouldn't sell yourself short. Surely there's been another man who's told you that."

She lowered her gaze. "Not for a long time."

She'd originally thought David found her attractive, but then discovered he really saw her as some kind of ugly duckling he needed to turn into his own version of a swan. Jake had brought her to Surfside Beach for a break from the last few days of uncertainty. But more than that, Gracie wanted a break from the years since David, years where she'd guarded her heart and never let anyone close.

But why should she trust Jake? He and David both came from the same kind of world—one where people didn't speak with accents, didn't wear blue collars, and vacationed in posh resorts of foreign countries—not in the modest neighborhoods of the relatives who worked at those posh resorts.

"Then someone's missed an incredible opportunity." His voice lowered, barely audible above the faint stirring of the car's engine. His green eyes turned a shade darker, like the peel of an almost-ripe avocado. The seriousness of his gaze commanded her attention. "When I called you this morning, I said I wanted to apologize for putting you in an awkward position last night."

She needed to jump in and rescue him from saying things that would make them both feel awkward. "Jake, you don't need to apologize. I—"

"I'm not going to apologize, Gracie."

"You're not?" Surely her elevated heart rate must be affecting her hearing.

"Can't you tell, Gracie? After I told you about the City Council's upcoming vote, I planned to just write you off. But I couldn't. And not because of anything extraordinary. Just because of who you are." He smiled at her with a sincerity that even the nagging whisper in her head couldn't deny. "You convinced me that not only was your school worth saving but you were worth getting to know better. I hadn't set foot in a church in almost a decade until last night. I came because of the school you created from nothing. I came because of you."

"Jake, that's not because of me, that's because of God. He puts people and circumstances in our lives for a reason." As the words rolled off her tongue, a light clicked on for Gracie as surely as if she had tripped an entire box of breakers.

"What?" Jake tilted his head and stared deeply at her, studying her face. "You look like you have more to say."

"Well, maybe I just answered my own question. I've spent the few days so worried about the circumstances surrounding you and *El Centro* that I forgot He's in control." Gracie could hear the animation coming back into her voice, like the moment in The Wizard of Oz when the scene changes from black and white to glorious color. "Maybe He's put you in my life for a reason. Maybe I needed you to show me those new properties, to push me out of my comfort zone and into a new direction. Maybe it's the start of a new and wonderful chapter for El Centro."

"It certainly could be, Gracie. I don't know much about God, but I do know the place we found today is a great location for you to both live in and teach. And maybe there's more. If there's one thing I've learned recently, it's that good friends are a gift, especially when times are uncertain."

Jake's hand rested back on the gearshift. Gracie reached out and covered it lightly with her own. She couldn't deny his observation. She worked so much that she had more acquaintances than true friends. But the butterflies fluttering in her stomach seemed more than just friendly.

"*Sí. Todos necesitamos amigos.*" She smiled, ready to release the apprehension that had dogged her for days, then remembered she needed to translate. "We all need friends."

The three quick raps on the window, each progressively louder, were a calling card Gracie did not want to receive. Even with her back turned toward the window, Gracie knew she'd just been caught.

"Graciela? Is that you?" Gloria's voice sounded muffled through the glass. Although technically asking a question, no quizzical inflections punctuated the sentence. Gloria already knew the answer.

Gracie turned around and punched the button to lower the window, wishing she could face any music other than her sister's. "Hi, Gloria. How's your afternoon at the beach?"

Gracie tried to keep her voice from taking on the tone of a teenager coming in after curfew.

"Oh, it's been good. Peaceful. Lots of sun." She lowered her head and looked straight across the small cabin at Jake. "But walking back to my car, I've noticed some storm clouds rolling in."

The only chill in the early summer air Gracie could sense came from directly outside the passenger door. "I see."

Gracie didn't want to discuss this right now, not while she could still remember the closeness she and Jake just shared. "Jake was about to drop me off for a little R&R with you, but since you're packing up, I guess I'll just find something else to do."

"Well, Mamí is making fresh tamales tonight for the church fund-raiser tomorrow. She'll need all the help she can get. Why don't we all meet at Huarache's?" Gloria popped her head through the window opening. "I don't know how it is in your family business, Mr. Peoples, but in ours, we all pitch in. When you're cooking, you can get distracted easily. If you mess with the recipe, things won't turn out how you want them to. It's good to have someone who can keep you from making a mistake."

Gloria's raised eyebrows and knowing smile only underscored the true meaning of her carefully chosen words. Gloria had smelled a rat early on in Gracie's relationship with David. She wanted Gracie to know her radar was on high alert again.

"I'm going home to take a shower and wash this sand off, and I'll call Mamí to let her know what the plans are. See you both around six." Gloria tapped the car door with the palm of her hand. It reminded Gracie of a judge's gavel after the verdict. There would be no pleas for leniency, no appeals.

As Gloria walked back to her car, Gracie could only shake her head. "You must think my sister is nuts."

"Not at all. I think she's one of the shrewdest negotiators I've ever faced. So, it seems we have plans tonight." Jake rolled up the window from the button on the driver's side of the truck, then shifted the transmission into gear. "I have a sister, too, you know. She and Gloria could fight for the front-row seat at Overprotective Siblings Anonymous."

The way Jake took Gloria's suspicion in stride eased Gracie's discomfort. "Well, what do you want to do now? It's only three-thirty."

"Would you mind if I dropped you off at your place, then came back to get you around five-thirty? I'd planned on reviewing my presentation for the board tonight, and if I'm going to be facing the Garcia family instead, I need to go to the office and get some work done."

"Sure." The time would give her the opportunity to compose herself before seeing her parents and Gloria.

Gloria...

Frustration and a little bit of anger mixed in Gracie's emotional pool. No matter how hard she'd tried not to, in Gloria's unbending presence, Gracie wound up feeling like a high schooler going to the prom who needed approval to stay out past curfew.

It didn't take long to drive from Surfside Beach to *El Centro*.

Jake pulled to a stop in the small parking lot. "Don't worry. Everything will be fine. It's working out for your school. This will work out, too. Remember what you said earlier?"

"Oh, I remember," Gracie said as she gave the door handle a gentle tug. "But in our family, we've always joked that Mamí has God himself on speed dial. She's probably giving him an earful right now."

"Don't worry, Gracie. I've met plenty of parents before."

"Maybe so." She got out of the car. "But were any of them Mexican?"

He shook his head. She had him there. Experience—and even a law degree—would be no match for a mama from Mexico.

"YOUR GRANDMOTHER HAS left several messages for you." Jake's administrative assistant, Anne, stopped him before he even reached his office.

"Thanks. Did you get my voice mail about the letter of recommendation for Gracie Garcia?" He thumbed through the short stack of pink while-you-were-out messages Anne had thrust into his hand.

"Yes, Jake. I've already drafted it and faxed it over to Melissa Miller's office."

"Great." Concentrating on tomorrow's presentation would come more easily now that he knew Gracie was taken care of. Jake tossed his laptop bag on the brown leather couch near the office door.

He would check on Nana, then get to work. He sat on the other end of the couch and pushed Nana's speed-dial button on the phone that sat on the nearby end table.

She picked up after only one ring. "Jake, where have you been?" Her voice did not contain any trace of its usual sunshine.

"Good afternoon, Nana. Is something wrong?" "I've been calling you for hours. Did you turn off your cell phone?"

Jake dug in his pocket. The phone didn't come to life when he pressed the button. "Looks like the battery died."

No wonder he'd had such a pleasant afternoon—no distractions. Except for Gracie and her charming smile, that is. How strange that in less than a day's time, he'd gone from thinking of Gracie as a nuisance—a roadblock to his personally constructed plans—to thinking of her as a friend.

"Well, I've been talking to Milton Brashear, and things are not looking good for tomorrow. Sam Pennington has gotten his little group on the board together and he's finally managed to convince them to vote against you."

Great. Sam Pennington had been Jake's father's best friend. No doubt Sam had been told every story Jake's father had concocted. With details.

"Nana, I thought you and Milton were working on him." He'd felt so confident this morning after helping Gracie find a suitable place to move. Once again, he'd tried to save everyone else and forgotten to save himself.

"We tried, Jake. Milton's had lunch with him three times in the last two weeks. Last week, he said he had concerns, but ultimately felt the company needed to remain headed by someone in the family for stability's sake in these crazy economic times. Today, he told Milton he'd thought about your father and changed his position."

"He thought about my father, Nana? That figures. Even in death, the old man is still at the forefront of everyone's mind."

He ran a hand through his hair and sank back uneasily into the office sofa. Like this situation with the board of directors, the cushions didn't have much give to them.

Jake looked at his surroundings, remembering how when he'd first returned to town, he'd redecorated this office, stripping the walls and the floors bare. Nothing remained of his father's choices. Nothing except a board of directors that, over the years, had seen Johnny Peoples turning his broad back on his only son.

"If I hear anything more, I'll call you. Please keep your phone on, okay?"

Her sigh was full of resignation. If Diana Powell Peoples couldn't fix this mess with her connections and years as the matriarch of this family, Jake knew there wasn't much hope.

"I will, Nana. Thanks for the heads-up." Disconnecting the call seemed like the perfect metaphor for his feelings. He now felt completely uncertain about tomorrow's meeting. His heart pressed hard and heavy inside his chest. A few months ago, Nana convinced him to leave Austin's memories behind and come back to Port Provident. She'd convinced him he could make a fresh start in his childhood home. She'd always believed in him, just as his sister Jenna had always believed in him. But apparently no one else in Port Provident did. He didn't know if he even could believe in himself anymore.

"I BELIEVE YOU'RE READY to move on to the next level, Margarita." Gracie said as she closed a workbook of basic English grammar lessons. "You've been a very quick study."

"Thank you, Gracie. I've been practicing a lot with Manny after work. We are only speaking English at home now so we can get better." The student, old enough to be Gracie's grandmother, beamed with pride. Even the bun of steel wool-colored hair atop her head shone.

Gracie pulled a red paperback from the corner bookshelf. "This is what you'll need for the next class. We will use dialogues for most of the lessons."

"So, I can start coming to the Tuesday morning class now?" Gracie nodded. Their tutoring sessions outside of El Centro's Level One class had clearly paid off.

"What's the matter, Gracie? You look worried. Do you think I won't be able to keep up with the new group?" Margarita's wrinkled forehead creased further with concern. "I saw you on the news the other night. Is that the problem?"

Gracie had tried to keep up a brave face these last few days with her students. And now that she'd found the new building downtown, she felt even more bothered that she couldn't release the trepidation that clutched her mind and heart at the most unexpected times. But a student like Margarita brought it all home—a grandmother who achieved her lifetime goal of getting a visa and reuniting with her precious children and grandchildren—only to find out she couldn't really communicate with them.

Gracie would never forget being new to America, without the skills to communicate. She'd never forget being at the bottom of her class until a teacher believed in her and helped her get the language skills she needed. There were so many stories like her own, and she'd grown up in a community of good people who wanted to better their lives, but just needed someone to believe in them— that's why Gracie had opened the doors of *El Centro por las Lenguas*.

Without her, they'd lose their momentum.

But without students to help and teach, she'd lose a piece of who she was.

The Center for Languages existed for people like Margarita. What would become of the Margarita de Leons, the Pablo Moraleses, and the Juan Calderons of Port Provident if Gracie couldn't make the numbers add up, and instead had to close her doors in just a few days' time?

A sinking feeling gripped Gracie's stomach. Too many people needed her to find a way. "I could use your prayers right now, Margarita. There's a lot going on."

"*Sí. Yo sabe.*" Margarita lapsed into the familiar comfort of Spanish and patted the seat of the green plastic chair next to her. "I know, Gracie. I heard about what the City Council is trying to do to you. I saw you on TV with Angela Ruiz. Gracie, *maestra*, you must remember God has a special spot in his heart for teachers. *Jesucristo* himself answered to 'Teacher' from the disciples."

When Margarita put her arm around Gracie's shoulders and squeezed, gratitude flowed like a balm over Gracie's raw nerves. It felt as if she was getting advice from her own *abuelita*, who lived so far away.

"He has not forgotten what He has called you here to do. When one door closes, He always opens another."

"I've heard that so many times in my life, Margarita. And even though I know I should trust in His plans, I am filled with fear over money and the possibility of moving, and..."

And Jake. Gracie knew it didn't take much for her thoughts to turn to the island native with the eyes like a Caribbean surf. But she didn't dare admit that to her student. She could barely admit it to herself.

"Well, *maestra*, it sounds like you need to remember the story of Queen Esther. Becoming part of the royal household wasn't in her plans. But she helped save her people because she had been chosen, as she said, 'for such a time as this.'"

Margarita picked up her black patent-leather purse as she rose out of the seat. "Maybe it's your time, Gracie." The older woman leaned over Gracie and hugged her tightly. "Be bold."

And with that definitive proclamation, Margarita walked out of the classroom. Sunshine broke through the clouds in her heart. Her time was now. She panned her gaze over to the door of her small office. Inside were the calculators and spreadsheets she would use to craft a budget for a time like this.

She would save her school and the dreams that depended on it.

The rest of Jake's afternoon passed with a slow sense of desperation. He couldn't focus on the work scattered across his desk. What did it matter, anyway? Sam Pennington was determined to see the rectangle of varnished oak become someone else's desk, effective tomorrow.

Jake couldn't sit around just thinking about the upcoming showdown. He needed to do something. He needed to feel as if control of his life wasn't slipping through his fingers like the sand on the beach where he'd always gone to think.

Jake turned his gaze to the left, then swept it slowly right. This had been his father's office. Even though Jake had moved his father's décor out—except the couch—and his own few furnishings in, the room still felt foreign.

As if it wasn't his own. As if it would never be his own.

A familiar memory came flooding back in Jake's mind with a strength that hadn't hit him since high school varsity football. He'd needed something to call his own back in those days, too. And to achieve it, he'd left town for Austin. Looks as though he'd be heading back tomorrow, once Sam Pennington got his way. He couldn't stay in Port Provident—not without a job.

He had creditors to pay as part of his recent settlement. He would have to make good on those obligations somehow. And he couldn't do it here, surrounded by the gossip and speculation that seemed to go hand in hand with life in a small town.

Jake yanked open the drawer to his desk. He stuck his hand inside without looking and closed his fist around a set of keys. Before Nana's call, he'd planned to go home and practice his presentation for the board. But maybe he needed to face the truth and spend his time working on other details.

Like packing a suitcase, putting some gas in the tank of the truck and getting ready to once again be forced out of this too-small town and its too many memories.

Jenna's white Toyota blocked Jake from parking in his usual spot next to the carriage house. He looked up and saw his sister bouncing his oversized black suitcase down the front stairs.

"Hey there, big brother!" Jenna waved her free arm in an enthusiastic greeting. "I got Nana to let me in."

"What are you doing?" Jake shook his head as he called out to her. "I'm going to need that."

"I'm giving it back, silly. You told me the other day I could borrow it for the cruise. Mitch and I leave a week from Saturday. I'm going to start packing now so I'm not rushing at the last minute, as I always do. I'm tired of throwing everything together like a tornado and then realizing I forgot my toothbrush. In the middle of the ocean, I can't just run down to the store and pick up what I need."

Jake stopped at the bottom of the stairs, blocking Jenna's path to her car. "Well, you'll need to pick up a new suitcase first. I'm taking that one with me."

His sister quirked one eyebrow high. "Taking it where?"

"To Austin." Jake reached for the black rectangle.

The usually chatty Jenna spluttered, trying to find her words. "But...why?"

"Just because." The words tasted bitter, like bad medicine. He wanted to say more, to confide in the sister who'd always loved him even when his parents hadn't, but he couldn't let Jenna know what was about to happen. Not after he'd promised to take care of the company—and her—earlier this very week. Knowing he would not be able to keep his word to his sister shamed him.

Jenna sat the suitcase on the stair behind her and looked straight at Jake. "Not good enough. You went to college and then you never came back. I'm just getting to know you all over again. I like having you around. I need my big brother. And a certain little person will need his or her uncle."

Like a small child turned loose on a pile of wrapping paper, Jenna's words ripped apart the numbness fogging up Jake's brain. "Wait a minute. You don't mean..."

Jenna's shy smile broke into a shining grin. She nodded her head. "Your little sister is going to be a mommy."

Jake stared at her as though he was seeing her for the first time. She wasn't just making those words up to get him to stay. The rosy glow to her cheeks looked too fresh to have been created by makeup.

He raked a hand through his hair. Jake tried to balance his desire to run far from his problems with the rising need to know the next generation of his family. But no matter how badly he wanted to support Jenna at this time of her life, and no matter how much he wanted to be this baby's uncle, it was out of his hands. Johnny Peoples had poisoned the cup years before. Jake looked at his feet and sighed. He couldn't be there for Jenna's baby because the only lessons he could teach were ones of failure and regret. A certain little person didn't need that. Jake wouldn't stack the deck against the newest and most innocent branch on the Peoples family tree.

"Congratulations, Jenna." He reached out.

Jenna leaned over to return what she interpreted as the beginning of a brotherly hug. Jake ducked her embrace and kept his head low. Maybe if Jenna couldn't see his eyes, she wouldn't know how much it hurt to know what would happen to him tomorrow.

His hand slipped past his sister and rested on the handle of the suitcase, tugging it out of the grip of the mother-to-be. "But I'm still going to need this."

Jake pulled into *El Centro's* parking lot and tried to adjust his attitude. The afternoon's phone call from Nana had started his emotional slide.

After running into Jenna and realizing that his father's disapproval— brought back to life by Sam Pennington—was going to keep him from knowing his first niece or nephew, he'd fallen into a funk he just couldn't pull himself out of.

Gracie appeared at the truck's passenger door and gave a quick knock on the glass. He hadn't even realized she stood there. The fog that had settled into his brain a few hours ago seemed too thick to clear.

"You don't look like yourself at all."

"What do you mean?" He didn't want to worry her with his problems. He'd caused enough stress for everyone around him—especially Gracie. He'd decided to leave after this evening with her concluded so he wouldn't add more stress by standing her up.

She deserved better than he could ever give. Gracie, the woman he'd just pledged his friendship to this very afternoon would be another person disappointed by him tomorrow once Sam Pennington finished resurrecting decades of gossip.

"You don't seem like yourself. Something's wrong." She settled herself into the seat, and Jake pulled out of the parking lot.

"Not really." Pride rose to the top of his throat, blocking the exit for any words to escape. "Now, how do we get to Huarache's?"

"It's not far from the church. Forty-Seventh and Gulfview."

"It's on Gulfview?" He couldn't hide the surprise in his voice.

"Mm-hmm. Why do you ask?" Gracie's eyebrows drew together as she studied him.

"Well, I..." He stopped speaking abruptly, embarrassed. "I've never noticed it. Has it been there long?"

Gracie's eyebrows changed position from confusion to amusement. "Only about twenty years. It's pink-and-orange stucco on the main beachfront street in town. How could you possibly miss it?"

"Good question. I seem to have missed a lot. I missed the signs that trusting a lying client would lead me into bankruptcy. And today it seems I missed the fact that my father's legacy will keep me from running my family's company." He pulled into the parking lot behind Huarache's. He realized that he did know this building—he'd just never taken the time to care about it. "I guess it's no surprise I missed a pink-and-orange restaurant every time I drove down this street for my entire life."

Jake kicked at a small pile of rocks in the parking lot as he got out of the truck. They scattered in a dozen different directions. Just like every dream he'd ever had.

He walked over to open Gracie's door, but she exited on her own before he could plod over there. She stopped his slow progress with a light palm on his chest. "Jake. Something is wrong. I can see it. Please don't close yourself off like this."

She gently tapped his shoulder. The soft touch reached through muscle and skin, around to his heart and pride. The stone inside began to waver like a palm tree facing the winds of a hurricane.

"It just hasn't been a good day, Gracie." He'd given her the background over their snapper lunch, but if he now started talking about the fact he was going to be the first John Edward Peoples in Port Provident history not to receive a vote of confidence to head the family company, she'd see right through him.

Gracie would know what his father always said. She would know the fraud he must truly be.

The light in her eyes dimmed as she spoke. "You spent most of your day with me. I don't understand."

His preoccupation with his own issues had prompted him to speak without thinking. Gracie had no way of knowing the phone call with his grandmother caused his day to take a dark turn.

She didn't know he'd made his sister cry on what should have been one of the happiest days of her life.

She didn't know that his hours with her filled his afternoon with the only pure sunshine in this gloomy day.

"It's not you, Gracie. It's me. I promise."

"What does that mean, Jake? Why are you using some cheap breakup line?" Her voice started strong, then trailed off.

If she hadn't been standing next to him, he would have missed the last phrase entirely.

But when she found out that he couldn't even save his own job at his own family's business, she wouldn't trust anything he said to help save hers. And when she realized he had no power to help her, they would go their separate ways in just a few hours.

Jake leaned against the rear bumper of the truck, trying not to think of tomorrow. "I had to let go of a dream this afternoon."

"What do you mean?" Her voice sounded as soft her floral fragrance that drifted on the breeze. Her gentle presence somehow comforted him.

He could hold back his thoughts from Nana and Jenna, but for some reason, not from Gracie. "My grandmother called. She's been tipped off that the board will not vote to confirm me at tomorrow's meeting." His ears ached at the sound of his own words.

Gracie's expression turned serious. "You sound so sure of it. Nothing's final yet. They haven't even heard your presentation."

"My father's best friend has gotten enough votes to block me. Even from the grave, my father's mistrust still follows me all over this town. All my life, my father kept me at arm's length from everything that meant anything to him. Once Sam Pennington reminds the board that my father didn't want me as part of his life or his company, I see no reason for the vote to go in a different direction from what Nana said earlier." Jake wanted to pull away from her intense stare, but her eyes followed his.

"So you're going to allow my business to be ruined for nothing? You're going to allow your family's business to be run by someone else?" She pulled away when Jake reached out to take her hand. "No. That's not the Jake Peoples I've come to know."

"Then you don't know the real Jake Peoples." The distasteful words practically spit out of his mouth. "Tomorrow, I'll be the first one in four generations to be shown the door from Peoples Property Group. First, my own law office, now this. The only thing it seems I know how to do is fail, Gracie."

A large family's laughter carried on the wind all the way from just outside the restaurant's front door. Their good-natured conversation prodded Jake like a white-hot poker. His family never had moments like that.

He couldn't recall his mother, father, sister and him ever laughing together in that way. Jake's jaw clenched.

He reached out a hand, without thinking, and slammed his palm into the side of the truck, barely missing Gracie. The sting of skin on steel hurt, but not as much as the memories.

"What are you doing, Jake?" Gracie gasped.

"I don't know." His breathing came heavy and short. "This wasn't how things were supposed to go. I was supposed to get it right this time."

The wind swirled gently around the parking lot as the sun began to set, framing Gracie's hair in gold.

"You know, Gracie, I think I'm not good company tonight." He knew canceling on her right here was cheap, but maybe she needed an introduction to the same Jake everyone else appeared to know.

"No, you're not leaving." Gracie replied. "My family's expecting you. You say you let down your family when things didn't work out for you in the past—well, you're not going to let down mine tonight." The determination in her voice could have intimidated a line of Army generals.

"Gracie, I'm not trying to..." She cut him off.

"That's right, Jake, you're not trying. You're bailing on *mi madre*, who's counting on an extra pair of hands tonight. You're resigning yourself to being kicked out of your company before you even give your presentation. You're giving up on yourself because of the expectations of someone who isn't even alive anymore." She stared straight at him, brown-velvet eyes full of concern. "And you're running away from me after you promised your friendship and your help in saving my school."

She pulled back, swiped her hand in the air dismissively, then began to walk toward the short stucco annex off the back of Huarache's main building.

Jake wanted to reach out and grab her hand, to hold on for a moment. But by the time he'd sorted through his thoughts enough to act on them, Gracie had already made it to the door. The hinges squeaked open, then a second later, the pink door slammed shut with a metallic thud. The silence in the night air wrapped around him. The laughing family had found their way inside and were probably sitting down to a good meal. Gracie had gone inside to her family, as well.

But Jake remained in the parking lot, on the outside as usual. He looked at the door Gracie had just walked through, then looked at the keys in his hand. It was time to go home and get ready to face tomorrow. Gracie Garcia was just one more missed opportunity in the life of Jake Peoples.

"AREN'T YOU MISSING someone?" Juanita Garcia looked up as soon as her youngest daughter walked in. "Your sister told us you were bringing a friend tonight, Graciela." Her mother's eyes sparkled with mischief as her arms rested almost elbow-deep in masa, the ground corn dough that formed the chewy exterior of a tamale.

"No, Mamí. Something came up." Like a complete and total turnaround from the self-confident Jake she thought she knew.

Gracie couldn't explain what had happened to Jake tonight. How could one phone call bring about such a change in a person?

"It tells you a lot about a man if he's afraid of tamale-making." Juanita Garcia's warm, throaty laugh—a sound Gracie had always loved—rippled through the room.

"I don't think it's that, Mamí. I wish I really knew what happened. Earlier this afternoon, he helped me find a new location for the school that will work if I get the grant, then we had lunch and ran into Gloria on the beach."

Gracie walked to the prep table and picked up a stack of dried corn husks, placing them in a bowl of water for softening. "Then tonight, he picked me up to come here and he wasn't himself."

Gloria walked through the side door, carefully balancing an assortment of spice bottles in each hand. "Where's Jake?"

"He's not coming," said Gracie and her mother at the same time.

"*Qué*?" The bottles rolled out of Gloria's arms and across the countertop with a thud that punctuated her simple question.

"I really don't know, Gloria." Gracie reached in her mother's bowl and grabbed a hunk of pliant white dough. "It feels good to do something productive instead of worrying. I've done enough of that this past week. First about the school, and then about Jake. I'm done worrying. On to tamales."

The vaguely grainy masa squished between Gracie's fingers. Each round of flexing and working the dough released a little more of her frustration.

Her sister gave a gentle hip bump as she passed by on the way to her own station. "Well, if you're not going to worry about him, Graciela, can I?"

"You don't even like him, Gloria. Why on earth would you worry about him?"

Gloria moved a pan of cooked pork close to her and laid an empty pan alongside it. "What do you mean I don't like him?"

"Well, both times you've met him, you've pretty much torn him to shreds." A voice several octaves deeper than those of the three Garcia women came from the doorway. Jake looked pointedly at Gloria, who pulled at the large rounds of cooked pork until they became small strips in the pan.

"Jake...you said you weren't coming." Gracie tried to keep the surprise out of her voice. She didn't want him—or any of her family members—to know how her heart leapt when he spoke.

"Well, you were right, Gracie. I promised some people I'd be here. I seem to have blown a big opportunity with my family.

I didn't want to do the same with yours. And if I went home, all I'd do was think about more negative things."

He crossed the room in two steps and stood next to her mom. "*Señora* Garcia, how can I help?"

"*Bienvenidos*, Jake. Any friend of Gracie's is always welcome in our kitchen." Her mother smiled a knowing smile. She nodded at the bowl, indicating she would shake his proffered hand, except for the mess that covered her to the forearms. "You can help Gloriana shred the pork, if you'd like. Gracie's measuring out the balls of masa. But we will need something to stuff them with."

"I'd be happy to. Gloria, you'll tell me what I need to know?" Gloria's eyes lit with mischief.

Gracie knew that look from a hundred childhood pranks. "You're up to something, Gloria." She wished she knew just what was running through her sister's head.

"Me? Never." Gloria looked down at the pork roasts and began shredding methodically. She lifted her head and met Gracie's eyes, then began to giggle.

Gracie's own eyes rolled at her sister's silliness.

"I brought sodas." Gracie's father stopped as soon as he entered the room and looked from Gracie to Gloria and then at Jake. He didn't say another word to his daughters, and instead set the bottles of fizzy drinks on the nearest counter and then turned to Jake. "Carlos Garcia. You must be Gracie's friend—the one Gloria told us about."

Jake reached quickly for the outstretched hand and gave it a strong shake. "Jake Peoples. It's a pleasure to meet you, Mr. Garcia."

"The pleasure is mine. Please, call me Carlos." Gracie stood dumbfounded, watching the introductions she'd been so certain weren't going to happen.

"I thought you were heading home."

"I did head home. I even pulled up to Nana's gate. But the sound of your voice replaying in my head wouldn't let me drive any further." His knuckles looked white as he gripped the edge of the counter. "If I don't keep my commitments when times get rough, I'm proving my father right."

A different warmth began to come over Gracie, starting deep in her stomach, when she heard him say he'd thought about her words as he drove in the car. She spoke softly, wanting to keep the bubbling emotion out of her words. "I think you made the right decision."

"And now it's time to get to work." Slapping a black nylon kitchen fork on the rim of the shredded pork pan, Gloria cut in the conversation and assumed the role of taskmaster. Her grin gave Gracie hope that her sister would give Jake a chance.

Jake walked over to Gloria, fingers raised in a quick salute. "Private Peoples, reporting for duty."

"Your mission, Private Peoples, is to take this pork and to give it some shock and awe." She pointed at several pounds of freshly roasted meat.

"Yes, ma'am." Jake found two more shiny aluminum rectangles and set up a processing station that resembled Gloria's, then stocked one pan with plenty of yummy material with which to work.

"Don't forget your gloves." Mamí pulled a pair of clear plastic gloves from a box on the shelf over the sink. "Gracie, take these to Jake."

Instead of taking them to put on himself, Jake held his left hand out for Gracie to slide on the glove. "Gracie?" Jake gave a sincere smile at her hesitation to put the glove on his hand. "You're slowing down the assembly line."

"I'm going to need the masa on those husks very soon, Graciela. *Rápido!*" Juanita cocked an eyebrow straight at where her daughter couldn't stop studying Jake's smile.

"*Lo siento, Mamí.*" Well, really, she only felt sorry about turning away from Jake and walking back to the other side of the counter.

"So, Jake, I understand you're in real estate?" Papí pulled a bottle opener out of a corner drawer and began popping tops off the soda bottles.

Gracie could feel herself deflate like the whoosh of the escaping carbonation as her father blindly dove into the heart of Jake's struggle tonight. She couldn't blame Papí for making small talk out of the only detail he knew about Jake. But still, she wanted Jake to feel as safe talking with her family as she always did when they cooked together.

Jake continued to work at his assignment. "Well, Carlos, I am for now. But not after tomorrow. Is Huarache's hiring?" He held up a handful of pulled pork and laughed as he spoke.

It made Gracie breathe a sigh of relief to see him joking instead of stressing. What a difference the passage of a little bit of time could make. "You may consider this my job interview."

"I'm sure we could find you a spot, Jake, although we prefer to hire family." Papí clapped a wide hand, marked with the scars from years around knives in a busy kitchen, on Jake's shoulder as he passed. Gracie had seen Papí give Gloria's husband, Felipe, the same sign of approval so many times over the years before Felipe passed away.

He brought the last of the soda bottles to the table and started handing them out. "Gracie, I know you want the orange soda. Jake? Which flavor do you prefer? *Limón*? These are popular soft drinks in Mexico. I hope you like them."

"I think I'll try the lemon, Carlos. I believe I had one of these as a kid when we went down to Cancún on a vacation." He took a long sip straight from the bottle. "How many tamales are we going to make tonight?"

"Ten dozen, maybe a few more. They're always popular at the church fund-raisers. Lots of families like to eat homemade tamales, but don't always have the time to make them." Mamí squeezed between Jake and Gloria and removed a pan heavy with a mountain of tamale filling. "Anything worth having takes time and effort. A good tamale is no different, Jake."

"That's a good way of looking at it, Mrs. Garcia."

"Oh, you should call me Juanita. Mrs. Garcia is Carlos's *madre*."

She smiled that warm smile Gracie had known all her life, the smile that drew people in and made them immediate friends. Gracie hoped it made Jake feel at home in Huarache's kitchen.

A snippet of a popular song began to play from Gloria's cell phone. Gloria pulled off her gloves quickly and answered the phone. "How are you feeling, Cara?" Gloria pushed back from the table and stepped over to a corner of the room to talk to her patient.

"I think I'm about finished here, Juanita." Jake dropped the last few shreds on top of the pile in front of him, then removed the spice-stained disposable gloves.

"*Muy bien*! You can help Gracie spread this masa on the corn husks, then I'll come behind you all and add the filling and Gloria can roll them up. Then we'll start putting them in the steamer."

A large, aluminum mixing bowl, filled to the brim with masa, got pushed toward the open spot next to Gracie. "What's the best way to do this, Gracie?" Jake asked, moving just a bit closer to her than necessary.

This wasn't the first batch of tamales Gracie had a part in making. She knew it would not be the last. But she would certainly remember it as the most enjoyable.

Gracie retrieved a husk from the bowl of water to her right and laid it out before her. "After you get a softened husk, you reach in and grab a good handful of masa. Then, with your fingers, you work it out evenly—all the way to the edges."

"That's how you make them by yourself, Jake. When you make tamales with *su novia*, it's much better to work like this." Carlos stopped behind Juanita, wrapping his arms around her so that his hands slid between her arms and torso, making it appear that there were four hands preparing the corn and pork.

Gracie hoped Jake's Spanish wasn't good enough to realize that the word Papí used could be translated as "girlfriend."

A small flush of embarrassment prickled at Gracie's cheeks like the brush of a holly bush. She and Jake were nothing more than adversaries who were becoming friends. No matter how old a daughter got, a father could still embarrass her without even trying.

"Maybe you're right, Carlos." Jake came up behind Gracie. "That would definitely make it more fun." Jake's easy interaction with her family made her smile. David had only met her family once, and he had made it clear that he didn't have any fun at the time.

"Jake..." Gracie tried to catch his attention in order to get his help with the giant bowl of masa that remained.

He wasn't listening. Instead, he looked into her eyes as though he'd never seen them before.

"Jake?"

He brushed back a lock of hair from her forehead, wiping a trail of masa from the fine hairs framing her face. The hairs moved past his fingers with a light tickle.

"Gracie." He ran his fingers across the strands again, seeming completely lost in his thoughts. "Thank you."

"For what?"

She couldn't believe it could be this easy. She hated letting bad memories crowd her mind while her heart was feeling so light, but she had to be honest. David and Jake came from the same world, so Gracie knew this moment of having Port Provident's prodigal son fitting in so easily with her immigrant family couldn't last. She didn't want to feel those feelings of rejection based on her heritage again.

So Gracie closed that door on her heart tightly, like the lid of the steamer Mamí was using to cook and soften the tamales.

"For letting me see that not every family works the same way as mine. My father only cared about his business. My mother only cared about being seen in the right places. My sister and I had each other, but we never experienced what you have right here in this room, except for when we spent time with Nana."

"Cara's in labor. I need to head to the clinic." Gloria's interjection unintentionally broke the connection encircling Gracie and Jake. "You can take it from here, Private Peoples. Make me proud, soldier."

Heading out the door, Gloria returned a bigger version of the salute Jake had given her at the start of the tamale preparations. Gracie viewed it as a sign of approval. Just as he had revealed over time with her, Jake's sincere side won out over the strictly business façade he tried so hard to maintain. Gracie wished he'd put this genuine and fun part of his personality front and center instead of trying to be someone he thought everyone else wanted him to be. How could she demonstrate to him the value of who God created Jake Peoples to be?

"Jake, are you planning to come to the fund-raiser at *La Iglesia de la Luz del Mundo* tomorrow?" Mamí sealed another bag of a dozen tamales as she talked.

Of course he wasn't. Gracie knew that answer before Jake even spoke. Tonight's adventure in Hispanic culture had to be a one-time thing, a break to keep Jake's mind off what lay around the corner for him tomorrow. Jake walked over to the sink, turned on the water and began washing his hands.

"What time does it start? I'd like to come."

Gracie's jaw dropped. She couldn't believe what she just heard. She hoped no one else noticed her shock. They'd think she was rude—and she knew better than to bring up the past with Jake around her parents, who were still angry about how their daughter had been treated years ago.

Jake raised his voice to be heard over the flowing faucet. "My board meeting starts at three o'clock. I don't know how long it will last. But since they've apparently already decided on the outcome, it probably won't take long." Jake turned to the paper towel dispenser in the corner. It hid his face, but not the flat tones of his voice.

"We'll be celebrating your confirmation tomorrow night at the church, Jake. Nothing is final yet." Carlos opened another soda, swapping out Jake's empty bottle on the table.

"That's right, Jake." Gracie's mother chimed in from her spot near the steamer. "If God wants you at the head of your company, nothing will stand in your way."

Jake nodded wordlessly.

"I can see that you're not convinced, young man, but Juanita is right. Look around you." Carlos spread his arms. "I should still be a cook in a small Mexican resort town. But here I am, in the greatest country in the world. I own my own restaurant. It's not the biggest restaurant in Port Provident, but I will have been open for twenty years next month. Plus, I get to work every day with the love of my life." Carlos crossed the kitchen and stood next to Jake at the sink. He placed his hand on Jake's shoulder. "That's God, Jake. If your dream is to run your family's company, it's because He's placed it there."

"Thanks, Carlos." Jake nodded again. "I wish I had the same confidence as you."

Carlos kept his calloused hand on Jake's shoulder, conveying fatherly approval through his touch. "It's not confidence, Jake. It's faith."

Three hours passed in Huarache's kitchen before Jake realized it. He'd stayed busy and the conversation had surrounded him so completely that he'd never even thought to check his watch. As Juanita sealed the last tamale in the last plastic bag, Jake found himself wishing the evening wasn't coming to a close.

From the moment he stepped through the door, the Garcia family welcomed him—even when they didn't have a reason to, since he'd almost bailed on them at the last minute. After spending time in her parents' presence, Jake better understood why he couldn't stop thinking about Gracie.

Carlos and Juanita had spent their years in Port Provident building a business, not because they were entitled to or because they would impress others, but because they desired to honor God's blessings in their lives. Gracie and her sister, the next generation, followed their parents' example.

How different from the way his father had run the Peoples family business and how Jake himself was raised.

"Jake, do you mind giving me a ride back to my place?" Gracie threw a sponge over his head and into the sink as she passed him.

He loved this relaxed side of her. Apparently, the time in the kitchen kept her from the worries about her business as well. "Of course. Happy to."

Jake would be grateful for the few more minutes to spend in her presence. He'd love to draw this enjoyable evening out as long as possible. "Would you like me to pick you up for the fund-raiser tomorrow? I can have Anne call you and let you know when the meeting is wrapping up."

"I only have morning and afternoon classes tomorrow, so I should be through about the same time you are." She finished wiping down the counter, then tossed another sponge into the side of the sink filled with sudsy water.

"Great." He smiled at Gracie just to see her shy smile back turn into a grin. It calmed the nervous quiver that had stayed in his heart since Nana's call.

"You ready?"

"Ready." Jake walked over to Gracie and stood next to her. It seemed like the right thing to do.

She didn't close the few inches of space between them as Jake realized he'd hoped. He couldn't think like that. Tonight had been a welcome break, but he had no certainty in his life after tomorrow. At this point in his life, he needed a friend and nothing more.

"Carlos, Juanita, it was a pleasure meeting you both." Jake extended his hand to Gracie's father.

"Jake, I know you had many reasons not to come, but we are glad you did anyway. It was good to meet you." Juanita gave him a quick peck on the cheek.

"I hope my tamales pass the test." Jake laughed, remembering the step-by-step tutorials Gracie's entire family had given him to make the simple, traditional food.

"I'm sure they will." Carlos replied as Juanita nodded in confirmation. "We'll see you tomorrow at the church, Jake."

Gracie gave the nail on her pointer finger a little nibble as her father spoke. "We've got to go, Papí. Jake has a big day tomorrow." She turned toward the door. Gracie seemed to be trying to step out of Huarache's quickly.

"You seemed nervous when your dad was talking." Jake stopped a few steps into the parking lot.

She looked down at her feet. Her words came out muffled as she bit down on another fingernail. "Parents. You never know what they're going to say."

Jake felt that there was more behind Gracie's words, but she stopped short of elaborating further. "I seemed to always have that problem growing up. My mother usually found herself halfway through a bottle of alcohol by lunchtime, so it was usually best that her slurring disguised her words. And my father, well, he'd never heard the adage about not saying anything if you couldn't say something nice. He was all too willing to elaborate on what he saw as my many shortcomings." Jake twisted the corner of his mouth wryly at the memory. "But luckily, neither of your parents seem to have any of those issues."

"No, not at all. They're good people. But sometimes they let their imaginations run away with them." Gracie's eyes looked distant, as though searching for some far-away memory.

Good people. Those words took Jake back to his earlier train of thought about Gracie Garcia and her parents. The Garcias came to America in search of a dream. Through hard work, Gracie had learned a new language, then fulfilled a dream to help others do the same. She opened a small business that changed lives and paid the bills. And her parents had achieved that American dream as well with Huarache's.

Gracie pursued a relationship with a God she knew personally and didn't shy away from making it a part of her life, a trait Jake could now see she inherited from both Carlos and Juanita.

Skeptical Jake even found that refreshing. He didn't know God in such a way, but he admired Gracie's honesty about her faith. Gracie impressed Jake. She hadn't been handed anything and hadn't squandered opportunities. Unlike someone else he could think of. In truth, Gracie was everything Jake hoped he himself could be.

He'd let too many good things go in his life. His new friendship with Gracie couldn't become just another casualty of his own streak of bad luck.

Chapter Seven

SOFT MORNING LIGHT peeked through the curtains in Jake's bedroom. The sun ushered in the day in which the prodigal son would learn of his redemption—or not.

If he could have pulled the covers over his head and pushed today's events off until a time when he could be assured of a positive outcome, Jake would have. But with Sam Pennington continuing Johnny Peoples's tradition of spewing venom as far as Jake was concerned, that day might never come.

And Jake knew he couldn't stay in bed forever. Dressing quickly, he stopped his nervous pacing only long enough to make coffee and pour it into a travel mug. He wanted to be at the office early and lock the door.

He now knew he didn't have much of a chance, but he did know himself. Jake needed to spend some time alone putting together the final plan.

Arriving at the office before any other employees, Jake reflected on all the classes in law school that stressed the importance of thorough preparations before going into the final arguments in a trial. He'd stand in a boardroom today, not a courtroom, but Jake Peoples felt he had as much on the line as any death-row defendant.

The morning passed, a blur of spreadsheets and notes from past presentations. He only stopped when his stomach insisted on some food, then went right back to where he left off.

Jake notched another line on the notepad on his desk. Forty-one.

Jake had checked the time forty-one times since returning from a solitary lunch at the sandwich shop down the street. He put his head in his hands as he realized only ninety minutes had passed.

A muscle in his neck—right under the base of the skull—cramped. Jake needed to release some of the building tension. He pushed aside an open file folder full of papers on the condo project and laid his head on the one available vacant space he'd created on the desk.

The sound of three insistent raps on his office door jolted through him. Eyes still closed, he tried to ignore the commotion.

"Jake? Jake?" The door muffled the voice, but every repeat of his name came through more loudly. "Jake!"

He lifted his head, fingertips squishing into the cool leather arms of the soft executive chair as he pushed himself upright.

"Coming, Nana." Jake raised himself unsteadily, still fighting off the fog that lingered in his mind after he opened his eyes. He caught a glimpse of the clock as he walked by.

Fifty-six minutes had slid past. Jake hadn't meant to fall asleep. He assumed sheer exhaustion and stress had finally caught up to him after a night of tossing and turning. The numb center of his brain thawed long enough for Jake to hope Sam didn't have a hidden camera in the office. He knew his father's close friend would relish documenting the interim

CEO sleeping before the most important meeting of his short and doomed career.

Diana Powell Peoples slipped in as soon as her only grandson opened the door just enough for her to fit through. Jake had always thought she looked younger than her seventy-four years, with very few wrinkles on her face. Today, though, every line etched into her skin seemed more pronounced. Could worry over this situation be aging her as much as he felt it was aging him?

"We need to talk, Jakey." Nana chose to pace instead of sitting. "Sam's arrived earlier than I thought he would. He's up in the boardroom, on his cell phone. We need to get up there. He won't be able to make hurtful calls with you and me sitting across from him."

"I hadn't planned on going upstairs quite yet."

"You don't have a..." Nana turned on the ball of her foot. "Jake?" She looked her grandson square in the eye. A few quick steps later, she folded Jake in her small arms.

Diana's birdlike stature did not affect her ability to give a bearlike hug.

"Nana..." He leaned into the relaxation he'd searched for all afternoon. "I just don't have a good feeling about any of this."

He never could lie to this woman who'd always believed in him. She patted his back, as she so often did decades before, when he'd been a little boy who had trouble getting back to sleep in the middle of the night.

"Me neither, Jakey. But we're going to get through this. No matter what happens in that boardroom, you're still my grandson, and I'm still glad you came back from Austin to try to make this company a better place. Let's sit for a second."

Jake followed his grandmother to the couch like a curious puppy. He needed these few minutes with Nana. He needed to admit to himself just how much it meant to him to be the family leader his father never trusted him to be.

"I want you to go up there and speak from the heart, Jake. You're just like all the men who've come before you—you like facts and figures. And I know you're proud of what you've put together in a short time on that condominium development over on Gulfview." She patted his hand. "But lots of people put together real estate and construction deals every day. I know that's not why you came back. Be honest with yourself and be honest with the board."

He could feel his breathing become less labored, something he hadn't observed since last night at Huarache's with Gracie. "But, Nana, how do I put something into words that I can't even explain fully to myself?" He exhaled strongly.

"I don't know. Only you know the answer to that. I've learned it's never a bad idea to pray." She stood up and squeezed Jake's shoulder. "I'm going to head up there and see what I can do before the meeting starts. Come up to the boardroom when you're ready."

The stately woman walked to the door and laid a light hand on the handle, then turned back to face her grandson. "No matter what, Jakey, I love you. Don't forget that."

Once she closed the door, Jake could hear only silence. Even his own thoughts fell to the wayside. He looked at his desk, covered in stacks of folders and reams of white rectangles with rows and columns of neat black ink. He wanted so badly to draw comfort from the sight of all his preparation. But instead, the view made his gut cramp, and left him more uncomfortable than at any time in recent memory.

Jake again took note of the quiet that surrounded him. John Edward Peoples IV stood alone. So very alone.

Echoes greeted the interim CEO as he took the first step off the elevator. The voices of the directors bounced off the polished marble flooring in the hallway to the boardroom. The amplified volume made it seem as though a hundred people crowded into the room, instead of the mere ten who would shortly be seated around the table.

Jake's stomach seized. He could feel the viselike teeth of fear clamping down. Never before, not even when he turned over his house key to help make restitution to his creditors as a part of his bankruptcy filing, did the acidic sea in his middle churn so violently.

The feel of a thousand ant feet blazing a trail buzzed over his skin. Gripping the pen and signing his name to the paperwork dissolving his law firm a few months ago hadn't made his hands tremble like this.

God, why did I come back? Why did I come back for this?

Jake had never directly questioned God in thirty-four years. And he didn't know why he thought God would answer him now. The Ruler of the Universe wouldn't have time to answer an off-the-cuff question from a perpetual mess.

God would spend His time with people who knew Him—people like Gracie. Gracie. Just thinking of her smile and her optimistic heart brought him a small measure of comfort. Facing the demise of her own business, Gracie never changed course. She showed him why her school was special, why her work was special.

And in doing so, she gained Jake's respect and support. If Gracie could do that, surely Jake could pull off a similar feat today with the board. Nana implored him to give honesty. And even Jenna's words from a few days ago came back to mind—don't forget what's important. All he needed to do was convince ten business leaders why he'd come back.

Too bad God hadn't answered his question yet.

"I thought I heard someone in the hallway." Milton Brashear, the president of Port Provident Bank and Trust, greeted Jake at the door to the boardroom with a solid pat on the shoulder. "Ready?" Milton meant the gesture to be reassuring—Jake could sense that—but instead it underscored what remained at stake.

"Ready." A less-true syllable had never been uttered in Jake's life.

"Everyone, Jake's here. Let's take our seats."

Milton ushered the prodigal son into the room. The thud of the heavy doors shutting reverberated deep in Jake's bones. No turning back now. Nana remained standing after everyone took their seat. As the only member of the family on the board, she customarily started the meetings.

"Welcome, everyone. We only have one agenda item today, the vote to confirm John Peoples IV, as the official CEO of Peoples Property Group. This will fill the vacancy left by the unexpected death earlier this year of my son, John Peoples III. Jake will present an update on the Provident Plaza condominium project on Gulfview Boulevard, then we will take the vote."

The matriarch sat quickly, as though she hoped to move the meeting along as fast as possible. She would not prolong the uneasiness either for herself or her grandson.

Sam Pennington spoke, his words deflecting Diana's poised introduction like an Army missile. "Diana, I don't think we need to see a presentation. We've all known the boy for years. Let's just take the vote."

A mutter worked its way across the room. It sounded like a childhood round of the telephone game.

"Agreed." Bruce Patterson, a local insurance agent who had served as a groomsman at Jake's parents' wedding, spoke above the din. "I make a motion we move straight to the vote. Do I have a second?"

"Second." Sam raised his hand with a dismissive flick of the wrist.

Jake swallowed hard. A lead weight worked down his throat. He could feel the stretching and burning at every inch.

"We have a motion to move straight to a vote." Nana's voice fell flat. "Jake, do you have anything you'd like to say?"

"Diana..." Sam used the woman's name as a warning.

She turned in his direction with whip-cracking speed. "Hold your horses, Sam. He deserves a chance to speak. You just took his presentation time away from him."

"We've agreed to a vote, Diana. You can't just keep propping your boy up." Sam would not give an inch. Johnny Peoples died in January, but his spirit of rancor lived on in the board members he'd appointed during his lifetime.

"Since you want to play by the rules, I move that we give Jake an opportunity to make a statement before the vote. Do I have a second?" She never took her eyes off her son's lifelong friend, even though she addressed the entire board with her question.

"Yes. Second." Milton waded into the fray.

From his chair at the head of the table, Jake surveyed every other face in the room. No one moved. A few looked down, unwilling to make eye contact. Whether they were keeping their cards close to the vest or just made uncomfortable by the verbal tug-of-war, Jake couldn't tell.

He hoped for the latter. He knew his odds were better if he could play for sympathy.

Nana turned away from Sam slowly. Jake knew she was daring the troublemaker to make her bare her claws again. "Jake," she said deliberately. "The floor is yours."

The significance of the moment overwhelmed him. This very floor might never be his again. He needed words.

"Thank you, Nana." He paused.

Breathe. Exhale. Breathe again.

"Ladies and gentlemen, thank you for coming today." Jake tried to stall with a little bit of introduction. "All of you knew my father, and most of you have watched me grow up, leave town and recently come back. For those of you who were surprised when I returned to Port Provident, I want you to know I arrived with the best of intentions."

Jake could see compassion in the eyes of many at the table, but only sharp daggers in Sam Pennington's cold stare. He resented every word out of Jake's mouth. "All of you work here in Port Provident, and you know what it's like to do business in a small town. Reputation is everything. And it seemed to me that Peoples Property Group had been coasting on our name instead of being at the forefront of shaping this town. I came back to change that."

Sam leaned forward and pointed straight at Jake, barging into the monologue. "No, you didn't. You came back because your own reputation got shredded in Austin. You're even more of a fool than I thought you were if you believe we're all going to buy your line, son."

Jake knew his father loved to spread stories about his naive mess of a son. He didn't realize how much his father's circle took them as the truth. Until now.

"It's not a line, Sam. I could have stayed to rebuild my career in Austin. I chose to come home to lead the family company after my father's death. I believed in my obligation to my grandfather and great-grandfather and the work they did here." He tried to keep his buttons covered up where Sam couldn't punch them.

"The family company? You're not really family. So, you can quit trying to—"

"You will not speak that way in my presence, Sam Pennington." Nana's gasp of breath came out more like a shriek. "Your last name is not Peoples, and you are not qualified to speak on who is or is not a member of my family."

The blood sprinted to Sam's face through the throbbing vein in his throat. His sallow skin turned crimson all the way back to the receding hairline. "Diana, I'm more than qualified to speak on who should run this company, and this boy isn't it. Jake's a fool who damaged Johnny Peoples's name before he was even born. I'm not going to stand by and let him damage Johnny's name in death. I could give my support to this company headed by a member of the family, but all Jake has is a big name he never should have been given in the first place."

Jake's heart rate increased to match Sam's. What on earth was the accountant talking about? He'd seen many sides of Sam, including pointed anger, over the years. But he'd never seen his father's best friend lose control.

He couldn't even hold a grudge over Sam's labeling him a lazy fool. Not until he found out what the rage-fueled speech truly meant. He'd had his suspicions for years. Now, he could know for certain—it was clear the same price would be paid no matter what.

"His mother was an alcoholic socialite who pawned her child from an affair off on my best friend. And how did Johnny get repaid? By a 'son' who rejected working at this all-important family company—until he botched his legal career." Sam banged on the table with his fist.

Jake swore the sound could have been his heart. Child of an affair? Not Johnny Peoples's son?

He'd often wondered if something like this would explain his father's coldness over the years, but no. It couldn't really be true.

Port Provident was the quintessential small Texas town. Gossip edged out high school football as the number one pastime. If Sam's allegations contained even a shred of truth, surely the information would have reached Jake's ears over the years.

Through all the questions and the doubts, he'd clung to the fact that no one had ever confronted him to his face with that ugliest of suspicions.

"Your name may read John Edward Peoples IV on your birth certificate. But Johnny Peoples isn't listed as your father. There's a blank line there. Haven't you ever wondered why? It wasn't an oversight. He wouldn't allow your mother to insult him in that way." Sam slouched in his chair, spent. His words came out in a surly growl. "Let's just take the vote, Diana."

To his right, Ken Potter shook his head. His confusion mirrored Jake's own. "There's not going to be a vote," his words came out slowly, framed in disbelief.

"What do you mean?" Numbness overtook Jake. He couldn't feel his mouth and tongue moving, even as they spoke the words. "The bylaws state that a direct descendent of the founder, John Peoples, must be CEO. If Sam's allegations are true, and you don't qualify, then the board must look elsewhere in the family or change the bylaws, neither of which we're prepared to do today." Ken's eyes looked pleadingly at Diana.

"You're right, Ken." Jake heard his grandmother's heart break with three simple syllables. "I don't know why Sam's bringing up these allegations today, but..."

"Diana, you know I'm not lying." She backed her chair from the table and stood. "There's no vote. Meeting adjourned."

Her voice trailed out on a heavy breath. Without another sound, Nana walked out of the boardroom her father-in-law, husband and son all had once dominated. Even her shoes didn't echo on the granite flooring.

Eight other members of the board followed quickly. No one dared to let out so much as a whisper. There would be time enough for hushed voices and gasps of surprise behind carefully shielding hands.

Sam Pennington stopped short of the doorway. He turned and looked at Jake. His mouth opened, stalled, then closed again. And then, the keeper of Johnny Peoples's legacy walked out the door, leaving only bitter memories—long past and brand-new—behind.

Jake stood alone in the boardroom over which he'd hoped to preside. The portraits lining the back wall dared to make eye contact with him. John Edward Peoples, John Edward Peoples II, and John Edward Peoples III all stared at Jake, unblinking. Swiftly, Jake grabbed the clear water glass from in front of him on the table. In his palm, it felt cool and smooth. Jake felt like neither.

He hurled the glass at the last oil painting with all the awkwardness of the young boy whose father would never play catch with him. He threw it at the canvas with all the rage of the young boy whose father would never say "I love you" to him.

Now he knew why. All those years of coldness. All those words of anger. All those instances without parental support. Johnny Peoples had never told Jake "I love you" because he couldn't.

Johnny Peoples had never loved Jake.

John Edward Peoples III took a direct hit just under the left eye. The tearing of the canvas as the painting in its gilded frame hit the floor, acted on Jake like the release of a grenade pin. Emotions exploded. Jake had lived a lie for thirty-four years. How could he ever trust anyone again? Fathers should protect their sons.

And so should grandmothers. Not only had he lost his family legacy today, the long-known-yet-buried secret caused

Jake to lose faith in the one person he'd always thought he could trust.

GRACIE SHUFFLED THROUGH the small pile of papers on her desk. Capping her red pen, she set aside the day's grading. She knew some teachers found paperwork like this tedious, but Gracie enjoyed the process. It gave her the opportunity to see the progress of her students. It always felt good to know she'd been able to help good people further their grasp of the English language as they sought to assimilate into this country, which had given them all—herself included—so much.

Now that she'd finished her work for the day, it was time to start thinking about tonight. She couldn't wait to see Jake and to hear about his presentation.

Normally, for a casual event like tonight's fund-raiser at the church, Gracie would just pull out a pair of cotton shorts and a casual, solid-colored T-shirt and pair it all with the official beachtown footwear: flip-flops.

But not tonight.

As she climbed the stairs, she mentally flipped through her small closet. She wanted to surprise Jake. She wanted to look like someone the CEO of an important local company would be proud to be seen with. She knew that, in spite of his doubts yesterday, the other members of the board would see through one man's vendetta and confirm Jake anyway.

Gracie pulled out her two favorite cotton sundresses and laid them carefully on the bed. She stared at them, brought over jewelry to match, then stared some more. Which would knock Jake off his feet? She giggled like a high schooler picking out a formal for a school dance, then realized she'd better watch herself. It was a casual church picnic with a friend. She'd attended hundreds of social events at the church— no need to treat this as anything other than what it really was.

Gracie decided on the teal dress with the flirty skirt, largely because she loved the chunky jewelry she could pair with it. Because accessories cost money she'd never had much of, she didn't own a lot of jewelry—but this set was a gift from Tía Elena, her mother's sister back in Mexico. Made of close to fifty pieces of deep-blue turquoise about the size of quarters, each minimally finished so that no two looked alike, the necklace made a statement. The sterling silver and red coral accents only added to the exclamation factor. She threaded the matching earrings through her ears, then added the bracelet and a ring that covered half her right ring finger.

"*Ah, qué bella. Perfecto.*" Gracie stood back from the full-length antique mirror in the corner and let the wide grin on her face become the final accessory. She twirled on one sandal-clad toe, letting the dress swirl around her. The outfit looked beautiful. It had come together perfectly.

Now all she needed was a phone call from Jake's secretary, telling her when he would arrive.

In the bathroom, Gracie touched and retouched her lipstick until she wore a deep crimson-and-rose hybrid created from multiple tubes of color. She brushed her hair seemingly a hundred times, then decided to plug in her curling iron. She rolled each segment and styled the curls simply by running her fingers through them, finishing with a light squirt of hair spray.

What else could she do while she waited? She expected Jake's phone call by now, and the nervous excitement began to overtake her body.

She twitched.

She fidgeted.

She paced.

And then she heard a thump-thump-thump from the heavy brass knocker at her front door. Gracie raced down the stairs so fast the clatter of her sandals on the wooden stairs echoed throughout the entire house, from upstairs living quarters to downstairs school rooms.

"Jake! I thought you were going to call!" In spite of her earlier admonitions to herself, she couldn't keep the smile off her face or out of her voice when she opened the door. The tiny bubbles of carbonated excitement that had been percolating inside her at a feverish pitch for the last hour all popped in rapid staccato as she took in the state of his expression.

She searched for the emerald sparkle that always drew her in like a magnet. Instead, only a dull, mossy haze glazed over his eyes.

"Jake? What's the matter?" She pulled the door fully open and stepped aside. "Come in."

Wordlessly, Jake shuffled through the door. His shoulders slumped, obviously weighed down by far more than his cotton button-down shirt.

Gracie stopped, reached out and grabbed his shoulders. "Jake, say something. What's wrong?"

"Everything."

The few remaining bubbles inside Gracie fizzled. "I don't understand, Jake." She couldn't let go. She now needed him to steady her as much as she'd originally thought he needed her. "Did your father's friend vote against you?"

"There wasn't a vote." His voice sounded flatter than the surf on a hot morning.

"What about your presentation?" She needed to know what he meant. Gracie couldn't translate what Jake now said into anything that made sense. "There wasn't a presentation. There couldn't be a presentation or a vote because the bylaws state that a direct descendant of the company founder must be CEO." His vacant stare darted down and locked with hers for a brief pause, then pulled up and connected idly with the corner at the back of the hallway ceiling. "There isn't even really a Jake Peoples."

Gracie grabbed the collar on his shirt. Her fingernails slid across the starchy sheen. The cool slickness of the fabric contrasted with the white-hot need she had to shake the information out of him. "You're speaking in riddles, Jake."

"I'm not my father's son and I will never be the CEO of Peoples Property Group. Sam Pennington saw to it that in death, my father dealt the blow he never could in life." His cadence picked up speed and his tone increased in volume. "I told you last night your family wasn't like mine. It's because my family lived a lie. Every day for the last thirty-four years. A lie. My father hated me not because he thought I was lazy or because I didn't do what he thought was proper, as he always told me. He hated me because my mother made him claim someone else's son as his own."

He ripped his gaze from the far away corner and shook off Gracie's hands with one pounding step backward. "I don't even know who I am, Gracie!" Jake roared.

Each syllable sounded less like the utterance of a heartbroken man and more like that of a bleeding animal. Gracie had longed for Jake's explanation, but finally hearing it took away all her own speech.

What could she say? No condolence seemed appropriate to give for being robbed of one's birthright. Maybe words weren't necessary. Gracie knew she couldn't erase his past, but she could provide a soft landing for his present.

Her arms went around his neck, and she pulled tightly, trying to signal that he could lean on her. There were no butterflies in her stomach, no feelings of excitement as there had been just a few minutes before when she'd heard Jake's knock at the door. This wasn't a hug of emotion.

It was a wordless statement of friendship and support. And the gift felt completely natural to give, with no further expectation. What kind of father would be so cruel to a boy he raised? Parenthood wasn't just genetics. When Jake deepened the embrace, the shared connection caused tears to well up in Gracie's own eyes. As her tears free, Jake pulled back ever so slightly. He leaned his forehead against Gracie's and linked his fingers through hers. With her head tilted just slightly, she could watch the wet drops fall on the scuffed wooden floor that had supported the weight of broken hearts for so many years.

THE BOISTEROUS SOUNDS coming from the church lawn scratched at Gracie's eardrums like a cat going after a carpeted post. After the silence in the car and the strained syllables at the house, it took her a moment to adjust to the fact that not everyone was dealing with the extreme emotions Jake faced.

For most people, this was just an ordinary Friday night with friends. Gracie held onto Jake's hand as they walked down the sidewalk toward the rows of tables covered with food and silent auction items.

Looking out toward the far corner of the church's property, Gracie could see a group of people holding "Save El Centro" signs and waving at oncoming traffic. Parked nearby was the same white TV van that had brought the news crew to El Centro earlier in the week.

She needed to find out what this was all about, but she didn't want to drag Jake over there and make him feel even worse about today's turn of events. A news crew might put a camera in Jake's face and take no prisoners. She had to spare him that further indignity.

Gracie stole a glance at Jake's profile. The tension made the muscle at the back of his jaw curl up. Maybe the other churchgoers wouldn't notice that Jake's usual smooth lines had been chiseled into hard edges, but she did.

But, in typical Jake fashion, not even a single hair was out of place. Nothing spoke to the turmoil within. Well, nothing but the silence between them.

"Jake! Graciela! It's good to see you both tonight." Marco Ruiz's face lit up when he saw them walk into the part of the yard cordoned off for the fund-raiser. Jake nodded.

Gracie decided to speak for them both. "*Holá*, Pastor. Jake even helped Mamí and Papí make the tamales for tonight." She gestured at the tables in the distance already covered with food.

"*Bien*. That means you're one of the family, Jake. Juanita doesn't let just anyone into her kitchen." He gave Jake a knowing wink.

Gracie felt certain Pastor Ruiz couldn't possibly know why Jake flinched a little at the mention of the word family. But if he did, maybe he could help. She needed to find an excuse to give them a few moments together. She didn't know if Jake would open up, but the pastor always amazed her with his perception. It couldn't hurt to try.

"There's Gloria." She spotted her sister setting up the table for the tamales. The perfect opportunity. "She looks like she might need some help. Be right back."

She squeezed Jake's hand before releasing her fingers from between his.

Please, God, speak through Pastor Ruiz. Bring Jake some comfort.

JAKE COULDN'T GET COMFORTABLE in his own skin. Ever since Sam Pennington's explosive allegations this afternoon, Jake hadn't felt like himself.

Whoever that was, anyway.

What if he never knew? His so-called father was in the grave. He hadn't spoken to his mother since he left Port Provident for college—when she, too, had left town. Jake sure didn't plan to degrade himself in front of Sam Pennington any further by asking for the dirty truth.

"Jake." Pastor Ruiz waved a hand in front of his face. "You're right here in front of me, but I can tell your thoughts are miles away. Do you need to get something off your chest?"

If he couldn't be honest with a man of the cloth, to whom could he come clean?

He knew Nana's etiquette books never would advocate unburdening oneself to a stranger, but he needed to talk to someone who didn't know him or his family—and wouldn't judge.

"Today should have been a good day. It should have been the day when I stepped up to the plate and finally took responsibility for my role in my family's legacy. I should have been named CEO of Peoples Property Group this afternoon. Instead, my late father's best friend used the opportunity to separate me from my family and my company."

The day's shame tasted bitter on his tongue.

"You never knew any of this before this afternoon?"

"I always knew my father didn't treat me like other fathers treated their sons. We definitely weren't Ward and Beaver Cleaver. I suspected something wasn't right, but I was always afraid to put a name on it." Jake couldn't hold the big question inside any longer. "If I'm not a part of my own family, Pastor Ruiz, where do I belong?"

Jake could hear the sounds of happy families in the distance, but the laughter couldn't fill the silent pause that lay between him and the pastor.

"Well, that's a question with an answer that is both simple and difficult." He stopped with deliberate thoughtfulness. "Your earthly family may have let you down. But your Heavenly Father knows you inside and out. He calls you His child, and He will not let you down."

Pastor Ruiz's dark mustache wiggled like a broom as he spoke. His words swept at the cobwebs of neglect and loneliness in Jake's heart.

Jake should have known this pep talk would come down to the same old tired Sunday school lesson. He decided to be blunt. "Of course a preacher would say that. I know that's how you see all this, but that's just not the God I grew up knowing."

Acknowledgment came in the form of a knowing nod. "Maybe so, Jake. But there's only one God. Not one for preachers and another for the people in the pews."

"Marco!" A slim woman with blonde highlights in her dark hair raised her voice above the din as she walked toward the grassy confessional.

Pastor Ruiz craned his head around to see the owner of the voice. "*Holá, Tía* Angela." He extended a beefy arm and waved. Jake looked more closely at the impending visitor. "Jake, do you know my aunt?"

Of course Jake did. Before him stood the wild card on the City Council who had staged that rally on the news and was likely responsible for the signs and TV camera he'd noticed in the distance tonight. He needed to keep his distance from that corner—and from Angela Ruiz's PR machine.

"Hello, Councilwoman Ruiz. You're the pastor's aunt?" Jake watched as Angela gave her nephew a quick peck of greeting on the cheek. Did everyone else have an open and loving family except him? So many friendly people surrounded him here—but he couldn't remember a time when he felt more in need of a friend.

"*Sí*. His younger aunt. Marco's father is my oldest brother. I'm the youngest of seven children. Marco here is five years older than me—it's been the running joke in our family for my entire life."

She smiled. Her relaxed joking and the happiness on the faces of friends and neighbors all around made Jake want to go home and sit in a corner. He didn't belong here. He didn't belong to his own family.

And he didn't belong to this "Heavenly Father" Pastor Ruiz talked about. If God did care about him, He wouldn't have let Jake live a lie for almost three-and-a-half decades. The numbness inside his mind slid away, replaced by the scarring lava flow of white-hot anger.

The muscles in his jaw clenched with a force that ground his back molars tightly together. "If you'll excuse me, councilwoman, I need to go find Gracie. Pastor Ruiz, thanks for your time."

Jake ducked around them and set out in search of Gracie. He knew he'd been abrupt, but if he didn't get out of here, he knew he was far too likely to explode on someone who wouldn't deserve that kind of treatment and the presence of the TV cameras scared him. He didn't want to talk to the media—he didn't even have the words to talk to Gracie. Jake needed to make his excuses to her. Her sister or parents would be able to take her home. He wasn't running away, but he knew she'd be better off without his baggage tonight.

GRACIE PERCHED THE last bag of tamales for the fund-raiser precariously on top of the pile covering the entire rectangular table. Although a small mountain of bags faced her now, at a price of only $ for a dozen, Gracie knew the bags would sell faster than snow cones at the height of summer.

Stepping back to admire her handiwork, she raised her eyes to scan the crowd but didn't see Jake anywhere.

"Oh, *hermana*—while I was at the post office today, I used my extra key and checked your mail for you. I think you've been waiting for this." Gloria lifted her purse off the ground and pulled out a slim envelope.

The faint nubbiness of heavy linen paper rubbed across Gracie's fingertips as she took the dove-gray envelope from her sister. Printed in a small black typeface in the upper left-hand corner were the words The Gulf Coast Educational Foundation paired with a downtown Houston address. She held its promise carefully in her hands.

"Aren't you going to open it?" Gloria prodded. "You've talked about this letter for weeks. Don't you want to know what it says?"

Gracie slid a finger in the space at the edge of the sealed flap, then stopped abruptly. "But, Gloria, what if it's bad news?"

"It's not going to be, silly. You've said all along how El Centro is the perfect candidate for this grant. It's going to be great news, and we're going to celebrate it here with everyone. Open it up or I will."

Gloria lunged forward, playfully reaching for the letter. Gracie ducked slightly out of her sister's reach and swiped her finger down the length of the flap, then up, popping it open. Gracie pulled out the letter, unfolding it with a slight tremble that she couldn't quite identify as fear or excitement.

She could see right away that below all the formal salutations, only a short paragraph made up the body of the letter. The Gulf Coast Educational Foundation got straight to the point of thanking her for her time in applying for the grant, but another recipient would receive this year's funding.

The letter fell from Gracie's hand. It tumbled downward, blown by the breeze like a lifeline bobbing away on the tide. She could see so many of her students across the churchyard—talking with friends, eating with family, playing with children. None realized the American dream had just become a little more difficult for them.

"What am I going to do, Gloria?" The worry on her sister's face compounded Gracie's hopelessness. "It's all over. I'm through."

"Through with what?" A deep voice broke through Gracie's melancholy.

"*El Centro*. I didn't get the grant, Jake."

"I'm so sorry. I'm the reason you're in this mess."

"You're not on the foundation's selection committee. You didn't do this," Gracie said flatly.

"No, but if I hadn't started everything in motion to get rid of nonprofits on Gulfview, you'd still have a building for a school and a home. You might not have your GED program, but it wouldn't matter that you didn't get the grant because you wouldn't need the money to move to a new location. This is all my fault, Gracie."

Less than twenty-four hours before, Jake had stood in her parents' kitchen and laughed and joked with her whole family. Now, she couldn't see even the smallest flicker of light in his eyes.

"Jake, you don't need to blame yourself."

"I do." He left no room for debate. "Gracie, I can't stay for the dinner. I'm sorry, but I need to go."

"Do you want me to come with you?" Maybe if they worked together, they could sort it all out. She wanted to hold on to the hope that not everything was lost.

"No. I just need to be alone. In fact, it's probably better for both of us if I just stay out of your life so I don't ruin anything else."

He let go and gave her one last look with hollow eyes. The first time he'd walked away from Gracie—when he notified her of the upcoming City Council vote— she'd been so sure she could change him. She remembered praying for the scales of judgment to drop from his eyes. Instead, working with her caused Jake to bring judgment upon himself. Why had that prayer been so misconstrued?

She'd prayed for a way to save her school. Why did all the doors continue to close?

And what about her prayers for a future with Jake? She'd always felt so certain that when she talked to God, a two-way dialogue occurred. Now, it seemed her prayers must sound to Him like a static-filled radio station.

Gracie didn't feel comforted by the thought of prayer right now. She felt alone. Abandoned both by the God who'd put the dream of El Centro in her heart and abandoned by Jake who—if she was honest—was beginning to steal a piece of her heart.

Jake lost the battle for his company today, but Gracie knew she had to keep fighting for hers—even as she now realized she'd have to do it all on her own. She squared her shoulders and took a determined step across the lawn in the direction of the protesters and the crew from KPPT-TV. She took a deep breath to clear her head and pushed toward the small crowd, where she could see Patti Cortez stepping out of the van, microphone in hand.

No Jake.

No grant.

No faith in her prayers.

She had to make a last stand with the only weapon she had left—the power of public opinion—or in a matter of days she'd have no home and no job, either.

Chapter Eight

THE LIGHT IN NANA'S upstairs bedroom winked out at the grounds below when Jake pulled his car back through the estate's gate after a long, aimless drive down beachside roads. The soft glow called to him like a homing beacon.

Jake parked his car and walked quietly inside the main house. He needed to talk to Nana, but he felt so betrayed that he didn't know how he could face her. Had she always known? He felt trepidation in every inch of his veins, but he couldn't turn around now. He needed to know.

"Nana? Are you still awake?" Jake tapped gently at her bedroom door. The century-old hinges swung silently as the door opened.

"Come in, my boy. I had a feeling I'd see you tonight." She walked to the sitting area off the main bedroom and perched on her favorite antique settee.

Jake sank into a tufted wingback close by and tilted his head back to where it rested on the solid upholstery. "I don't understand, Nana. Everything's such a mess."

"I'm not going to take Sam's tirade lying down. I need to pray about it some more before I figure out the best way to handle things," Nana said thoughtfully.

"Pray about it?" Jake tried not to roll his eyes. This isn't what he'd come upstairs for.

He already knew this praying nonsense didn't get anyone anywhere. He needed to look no further than sweet, God-fearing Gracie, who prayed with her whole heart about her grant money. All she received in reply was a letter telling her "Better luck next time."

"What are you shaking your head for, Jake?" Nana leaned in close and stared him down. He couldn't tell if she was trying to be playful or not. Something inside told him to go with the latter. "Do you have a problem with prayer?"

"Nana, God's got better things to do than to figure out a way for you to get even with Sam Pennington."

"I said I needed to know the best way to handle the situation." She sat on the edge of the settee, looking like a queen. "Your father would have been interested in getting even. But then, he never prayed a day in his life. And although he was my son, he led a miserable life. A relationship with God would have given some meaning to his days beyond dollars and cents."

"He had a company to run, Nana. I don't agree with how he treated people, but you have to admit the bank accounts didn't suffer while he ran the show."

Without replying, she rose and walked to the ornately carved mahogany bookshelf in the corner of the room. "Mm-hmm," she said, running her finger across the top of a section of older books, then pulling one out.

Diana Peoples stood in front of her grandson and put a small volume in his hands. Printed more than a century before, it felt slick to the touch, as though many hands had held it and turned its pages. The black letters pressed into the red cloth cover read "The Peril of Port Provident," above a dramatic engraving of a family. Jake assumed the book was yet another history of the Great Storm of 1910, the defining moment in Port Provident's history.

"Open it to chapter ten," Nana said simply. He complied, leafing through the pages and absently noting how much thicker the paper felt compared to the slick, mass produced sheets in contemporary publications. "Now, what does the chapter title say?" Her voice carried clearly, amplified by the high ceilings and shining wooden floors of the sitting room.

"John Peoples Prays to Put Port Provident Back on the Map," Jake read as dutifully as a student at a school desk.

Nana broke her dearly held etiquette rules as she sat on top of the coffee table behind her. Her grandson fidgeted on the cushion of the stately chair, uncomfortable under the weight of Diana's heavy stare.

She reached over the top of the book and tapped the top of the page for emphasis. "That man is just a legend to you. A story in a book that's more than one hundred years old. A name you've seen on buildings and plaques around town. But I knew him. He was my father-in-law. And he started a business when he was twenty years old that brought this town back to life. He built homes for people who'd lost everything. And he didn't do it because it looked good on a balance sheet. John Peoples started Peoples Property Group because he prayed about how to help his fellow citizens and God led him to the answer. His son knew that. His grandson rejected it. And it breaks my heart that his great-grandson doesn't understand it."

Jake's eyes burned. He stared at the letters on the page, unable to even blink. John Peoples Prays to Put Port Provident Back on the Map. Why had he not known this about the founding of the company? Had the distance between Jake and his father caused an even greater distance between Jake and the Peoples family history?

"What does this mean for me, though, Nana?" Jake felt like a child all over again, needing reassurance from his elders. He needed more than reassurance tonight. He needed answers to questions too bitter still to put into words.

"I don't have the answers, my sweet grandson. But I know Someone who does." She took hold of the book and folded it closed. "We'll figure it out. I told you, I'm not going to let Sam Pennington spread his vicious gossip about our family."

Her voice rang with the pure steel possessed by generations of Texas women. Jake knew if he hesitated, he'd lose his nerve. He had to lay it all out now. The hurt, the betrayal, the pain caused as today's daggers severed him from the only family he'd ever known.

"But you've always known it's not gossip, haven't you, Nana? He's telling the truth." The black cloud surrounding him blew a cold wind as he confronted the grandmother he'd always loved so fiercely.

Nana's breath floated away like a gentle butterfly. He could hear the exhale above the stark silence.

"Well, yes. I have, Jake."

"Then why didn't you tell me?"

He needed to hear the answer. An answer that, in his heart, he already knew. But hearing her admit that she'd kept such a secret from him felt like a punch to the gut.

"I tried to protect you. Your mother couldn't work through her problems—she just drank her way around them. I knew you couldn't rely on her." Nana paused and closed her eyes, always a sure sign to Jake that she was choosing her words carefully. "And your father clearly took out his anger at your mother and her infidelity on you. But you just needed someone to love you. I thought by keeping quiet, I was doing just that."

"All my life I knew something didn't add up. This is a small town. Everybody talked. Most behind my back, but some to my face. It hurt." The bitter bile of memory rose in Jake's throat. "I always kept my chin up by telling myself that they were liars. Because you wouldn't have told me I was your special grandson if I wasn't really yours."

Nana opened her mouth to speak. Jake held up a hand and cut her off. He'd never treated his grandmother with such casual disrespect before. He'd never felt he had a reason to before, either.

"I told myself they were all liars—and that for whatever reason, my father was the biggest liar of them all." Jake looked straight at Nana but didn't see her clearly with his vision clouded by years of hurt and anger. "It turns out you were the liar, Nana."

Jake pivoted, his leather shoes spinning slickly on the antique silk rug below. He turned for the door, unwilling to let Nana speak. He didn't want to hear her try to mount a defense. He'd heard enough for one day.

In fact, he'd heard enough for a lifetime.

Jake walked back to his apartment in the carriage house without another word to his grandmother. One thought kept running through his mind. Could the same faith that formed the bedrock of Gracie's family actually be at the core of the man who was, at least, his namesake? Could he find a way to truly know for himself?

He should have been thinking about his next move, what he would do from here. What work prospects did he have now? Where would he go in order to meet his obligations?

Instead, his mind couldn't focus on the here and now. It kept spinning with thoughts about the post-hurricane actions of the first John Edward Peoples, so many years ago. Jake's inattentiveness to everything around him caused him to catch his toe under the edge of the jewel tone-colored area rug. He tripped and landed on the plush carpeting. The fall interrupted Jake's inner turmoil and he surveyed life from his new, more lowly perspective. Jake grimaced as he realized, with a touch of irony, he had just been brought to his knees.

The wind kicked up outside, the howl reverberating across the windowpane. Jake didn't feel alone inside the small living quarters. Instead, he felt prompted, like a youngster being supported on his first bike ride without training wheels.

"I don't know how to do this. I've never really prayed before in my life. But I want to know how I'm supposed to make sense of today. I came back to lead my family's company, and now it seems I've lost my family and my company. And along the way, I made Gracie lose her home and her business. I don't want to be like that. I want to be like my great-grandfather. I want to help people build better lives. What should I do?"

Jake looked around, half expecting to see a sign that would let him know he'd been heard, but he couldn't make out much of anything in the dark carriage house.

The moon shone through the open curtains at the back of the small room. A few clouds began to gather at its edge. The gathering storm clouds made him think of the recent events in his own life.

The moon reminded him of his walk on the beach with Gracie. She inspired him. They handled life's curveballs so differently. When faced with losing his home and law practice in Austin, Jake filed for bankruptcy and left town. But when a similar situation literally knocked on Gracie's door, she turned to God, family and friends—and kept working to find another way to keep her dream alive.

Even now, when she knew the grant money wouldn't land in her bank account, she still believed that God would work all things out for good, as she'd so often said.

"Can you really make something out of this mess, God? Gracie seems so sure You have a higher plan for her. Do You have one for me, too?"

Again, no audible reply. Just a gentle reminder of another conversation with Gracie.

"I don't want to hear some fancy words you learned in a class for your MBA," she'd snapped at him in the condo parking lot. *"When you hear 'P&L' you think of a profit and loss sheet. I think of people and love."*

He'd gotten it all wrong. The measure of true success came in numbers of lives touched, not numbers of dollars in a bank account. Just as the chapter in Nana's book showed. *El Centro* wasn't a drain on the economy of Gulfview Boulevard, as he'd recently tried to convince the City Council. Instead, it was the only business in the area that generated the kind of profits that mattered.

The man he'd always known as his great-grandfather brought Port Provident back from ruin by investing in the lives of others. This special city didn't need another condo development. It needed personal development.

Jake got up off his knees. He owed a special person in his life a special apology, and then he had a phone call to make.

"Thank you," he whispered, dashing out of the carriage house like a firefighter en route to a rescue.

"BUBBLE BATH, TAKE ME away." Gracie poured a capful of lavender-scented body wash under the faucet of running water. The familiar floral scent soothed her nerves.

The whole day seemed so unbelievable. Losing the grant. Losing her school. Losing her home. Losing Jake. She'd only known him a short time, but his decision to withdraw from her life tore her heart like an angry bear's paw.

His last words to her at the church shredded her heart to ribbons.

Gracie knew she'd be rebuilding her life soon. Somewhere, there would be a new home, and somehow, a new school. She only wished she didn't have to add a new Jake to the growing list.

As though there could be another Jake.

In a short time, she'd come to appreciate him more than she'd ever expected. When he first knocked on her door, he was her enemy—an adversary from the other side of the tracks. But in spite of their differences, she'd found they had common ground. The wind crackled through fronds of the palm trees outside her window, and the first droplets of the summer storm released from the clouds above. Gracie wished her whole day would blow away with the gusts and the rain.

Gracie stopped the flow from the bathtub tap. She looked at the water and was struck by how, in such a short time, Jake had completely filled up her life in the same way the bubbly liquid took over the claw-footed bathtub.

On this night, when they'd both been given a rude awakening from their hopes in life, did Jake's thoughts race through his mind at the same warp speed hers seemed to travel? She didn't know, and his last words to her made it very clear that she couldn't reach out to ask.

The heavy sound of the brass knocker on the front door cut into Gracie's musings. She knew it would probably be Gloria, bringing cookies or brownies, or some other pity party-appropriate food purchased at the church fund-raiser. A smile crossed Gracie's lips. Chocolate within arm's reach would make the bubble bath even more of a haven from a cruel world.

She tied the knot tightly on her purple terrycloth bathrobe and walked down the stairs. With every step, the downpour outside intensified. "Hold on. I'm coming." Texas storms were known for changing from mild to malicious in just a minute's time.

"Jake! What are you doing here?" She couldn't believe her eyes. The water made his hair seem two shades darker, and beads dripped from the tendrils framing his face.

He still wore the dress clothes from his meeting today, and the cotton button down wetly molded to his every angle. Only hours ago, he'd said he was stepping out of her life. But here he stood, on her front porch.

What brought him back?

"I'm calling it off, Gracie." A crack of thunder popped from the storm cloud overhead. He drove all the way to her house to rub it in?

"I heard you loud and clear at the church, Jake. Our friendship is over. I know."

Jake took two steps closer. Gracie stepped back, both in confusion and to allow him through the door.

The clouds outside made the night even darker, and she'd only flipped on one light switch as she'd walked down the stairs. But even in the dimly lit entryway, Gracie thought she could see the emerald flicker that had been absent earlier today. Jake's eyes no longer appeared dull and lifeless.

He shook his head. "No, not you and me, Gracie. I made a mistake in saying that. But I made a bigger mistake in pushing the City Council for the Maximized Revenue Zone."

"What?" Gracie's eyebrows shot straight for her hairline. "I don't understand."

"I'm calling Carter Porter and asking him to withdraw the proposal. You can keep your school," Jake said.

Had she just taken a hit to the back? She couldn't catch her breath. Suddenly, as the old hymn said, peace like a river flowed. All the day's stress melted away, taking the worry of the whole week along with it. And she hadn't yet dangled even one toe in the warm lavender bathwater upstairs.

"I can keep my school?" She forced her arms to remain at her side instead of reaching out to hug Jake.

Gracie didn't want to overstep any boundaries. Everything today shifted from one extreme to the other so rapidly that it almost made her seasick.

"But what about your condo's swimming pool?"

"Well, the project's not mine any longer, remember? And without me, I imagine the company will go back to the original blueprint. The board never even listened to my proposal for the expanded amenities."

Gracie tore her gaze away from Jake and looked around the ground floor. She surveyed the classrooms, plastic tables in neat rows with folding chairs arranged in regular intervals. She paused briefly at her office, where her secondhand desk chair would support her for many days to come.

Gracie's wounded heart mended and swelled with joy. God hadn't misunderstood her prayers after all. He'd saved her school.

"Let's get you a towel. Wait right over there." Gracie pointed at the guestroom as Jake followed two steps behind on the way up the tall staircase. She went into the bathroom and grabbed the towel she'd laid out for herself. The bubbles that had piled up so frothily just a few minutes before had now all faded back into the water. But enough bubbles percolated through Gracie's bloodstream to more than make up for their absence.

You can keep your school, Jake had said. Could she keep him in her life, too? She didn't want to allow herself to think too hard about exactly what her heart meant by that.

When Gracie walked into the guestroom, Jake gratefully took the towel and began to roughly dry his hair, then wiped up the small puddle below him on the floor.

"I didn't mean to barge in on you like this."

"It's okay. I was just alone with my thoughts tonight. I left the church not long after you did."

The springs of the twin bed creaked as Jake sat heavily on top of the pink ring quilt covering it. "I shouldn't have taken my frustration out on you, Gracie. You reached out to me after reading that grant letter and I wasn't there for you."

"You were dealing with your own issues today, Jake. It's okay." Gracie leaned against the doorframe.

She remembered the hollow feeling inside when she'd watched him walk away. But he'd come back to her. That was all that mattered.

"No, it's not. And Nana reminded me of that. God puts us into the paths of others for a reason." He pushed still-damp hair out of his face.

She wanted to tell him that it would all be forgiven if he'd just say he didn't mean the part about staying out of her life forever. "Well, yes, He does. But that isn't what they teach in the MBA program, and you've made that clear before. When did you start listening to God?"

"When I realized that's my family's strongest legacy—not a company." Jake locked eyes with her.

Gracie could sense the seriousness in their clear green depths.

"Nana showed me a book tonight, written after the Great Storm of 1910. It talks about how Peoples Property Group got started. The company is a means to an end, but it's not the only way I can live out the vision of my great-grandfather. I am no longer part of the company, but I still want to be part of the work he was called to do—to help others build up their lives."

Gracie straightened up. Jake got her attention.

"You were right, Gracie. It's about people and love, not profit and loss." He stood and walked over to her. The room lit up from a full flash of lightning out over the nearby gulf. The accompanying thunderous boom made the house sway on its pier-and-beam foundation.

She reached out and clutched Jake. Gracie knew she would have even if there had been no storm. She wanted to hold onto him forever. She wanted to hold onto this feeling in her heart forever. All her life, she'd known she left her homeland to find something new.

When Jake said her own words back to her, she knew she'd found not just a friend, but maybe more.

ALTHOUGH JAKE WANTED to stay much longer and talk about the future with Gracie, he needed to take care of some important business right now.

"I'll see you tomorrow. I want to take you out on a real date." He waved as he ran off the porch and across the asphalt to where he'd parked his truck. Today's events tossed his future up in the air. He didn't know what he would do for a job once he cleaned out his desk Monday morning.

But what mattered most is that Gracie would stand by his side.

As soon as he shut the door to the car, Jake dialed Carter Porter's number. It went straight to voice mail. "Carter, it's Jake. Look, I need you to take the vote on the Maximized Revenue Zones off the table for Monday's meeting. It's not something I'm interested in pursuing any further. Call me if you have questions. If I don't hear back from you, I'll assume everything's taken care of."

He hung up the phone and drove back to the carriage house. Everything seemed to be falling into place. Jake loved it when a plan came together. Especially when he knew it was God's plan.

The phone rang almost as soon as Jake disconnected the call to Carter Porter.

"Jake?" Jenna's soft whisper sounded wet with tears.

"Jenna, I'm so sorry. I owe you an apology." He needed to make things right with his sister. He'd treated the news of her pregnancy exactly the same way his father would have treated a major announcement of Jake's.

"It's okay, Jake. I've been on the phone with Nana." She gave a weepy little hiccup. "It's not right what Sam did to you."

Jake pulled his truck into a parking spot alongside Gulfview Boulevard. He wanted to be able to give Jenna his full attention, not be distracted by the drive back home.

"No, it's not. But I'll be okay. I didn't know that at first, but I do now." A smile of recognition crossed Jake's lips as he spoke. "You were right, you know."

"About what?"

Jake watched the waves below get splashed with raindrops and remembered a few days back when Jenna gave him a stern warning in his office. "You told me not to forget the important things in life. It wasn't that I'd forgotten them, Jen. Until tonight, I never really knew what they were."

His heart broke a little for the person he had been, the person who had always struggled to live up to unrealistic expectations.

Jenna didn't reply immediately. "So what did you learn? What are the important things to you?"

"Family. Faith. Doing what you can to help others." Jake answered his sister swiftly and without doubt. "Being an uncle who cares. Jenna, I'm really sorry for how I reacted to your news. I want to be there for you and for the baby. I want to remember what truly matters in life."

"Really?" Jenna's voice peaked on the last syllable. "You mean that?"

Jake nodded, confirming it to himself as much as Jenna. "I mean it. I know that Sam Pennington's revelations mean I'm only your half-brother, but that doesn't matter to me."

Jenna cut him off. "It doesn't matter to me, either. You've always been my brother. You always will be. No DNA or gossip will change that. And I want my baby to grow up knowing that the Sam Penningtons of the world will not win in the end. You and me—we're family, Jake, no matter what anyone says."

"I'm glad you feel that way, Jenna. I don't know what I'd do without you."

"I know something you can do," Jenna said.

He'd do anything for Jenna, and he wanted to prove it to her. He wanted to build an extended family who laughed together and supported each other in good times and bad, just as the Garcias had. "What? Name it."

"Come with me tomorrow to my prenatal appointment. I've transferred from the hospital's OB/GYN practice to a midwife at that little birth clinic on the corner of Sixth Street, next to Provident Medical Center—and they have Saturday morning appointments. I scheduled it then because I thought Mitch could come, but I forgot he has to fly out of town for a conference. Will you come with me? They'll be doing an ultrasound. You can see your niece or nephew for the first time."

Why not? He could clean out his desk any time. He'd probably never have the opportunity to see Jenna's baby on an ultrasound screen again.

"Absolutely, Jenna." His heart leapt at the thought of being there for Jenna and her baby.

"Great." Jake could hear only smiles—no more sniffles—coming from the other side of the line. He would be there for Jenna.

This should have been the loneliest night of his life. Instead, he'd found his relationships and his purpose renewed. He'd found out the true meaning of really mattered in life—people and love.

Chapter Nine

JAKE PULLED UP TO JENNA'S beachfront condo just before eight o'clock the next morning and honked the truck's horn.

"Coming!" She opened the front door and shouted, then ran back inside. When she came back out, she was holding a purple notebook.

Jake watched as she ran down the sidewalk toward the truck. She still seemed just as fast as in her high school days, when she flew from one end of a basketball court to the other.

In some ways, Jake couldn't believe his little sister was having a baby. Truthfully, it was hard to believe she was actually married. He remembered when she used to play house in the backyard with her teddy bears and tea sets.

"Hey, little mama," Jake teased. "You ready?"

"Yup." Jenna closed the door to the truck and buckled up. "I'd forgotten my notebook. I'm keeping all my notes about the pregnancy in it. I don't want to forget a single second of it."

She flashed him a wide grin, full of pride and excitement. Jenna was so excited about every little detail pertaining to this baby already. Jake had no doubt she would make a great mother and that this baby would have the loving, secure childhood Jake himself never did.

The trip to the Provident Women's Health and Birth Center only took about five minutes. It was a small building on the far corner of the property that made up the Provident Medical Center.

"The clinic is in the front of the building, and at the back are four birthing rooms designed to be like a room at home. They're close enough to transfer patients quickly and efficiently in case of an emergency, but far enough away that you don't have to feel like you're in a hospital."

He had to admit, the oversized craftsman-style building surrounded by oak trees and flowerbeds full of pansies in bright shades of yellow and purple looked like a much cozier place to start a family than the stark, hushed hallways of the hospital next door.

Once inside, Jenna stepped right up to the sliding-glass window at the back of the waiting area. "Hi, I'm Jenna Carson. I'm here for my appointment."

The receptionist gestured at a clipboard on a small ledge. "Just sign in and your midwife will be right with you."

Jenna scribbled on the paper, then walked over to a wingback chair next to where Jake was seated. "Uncomfortable, big brother?"

Jake tried to scoot back from the edge of his chair and pulled back at his collar. "It's all so...female...in here."

"Well, sure. It's a women's health clinic." Sarcasm coated Jenna's words and she rolled her eyes at Jake in the universal look of sisters who thought their brothers were a little crazy.

"But I'm not a woman. I'm not even married to one. This is all new to me."

A brown door next to the small sliding-glass window opened. The midwife looked up from the chart in her hand. "Jake?"

Gloria Garcia Rodriguez's eyes shot white-hot sparks in Jake's direction. "What are you doing here?"

Jenna jumped out of her chair and clutched at Jake's arm.

The sparks in Gloria's eyes intensified.

"Jake, do you know Gloria? She's going to be my new midwife."

"Oh, he knows me," Gloria said flatly. "I'm his girlfriend's sister." The emphasis on girlfriend was unmistakable. She stared at Jenna with disbelief starkly painted across her face. "So, you've orchestrated another surprise for Gracie?"

The words startled Jake. He'd only asked Gracie on an official date last night. But Gloria seemed to have gotten other ideas. And something told him this wasn't the time or place to deny Gloria's suspicions.

"Who is Gracie, Jake?" Jenna looked back and forth between her brother and the midwife. "And since when do you have a girlfriend?"

The silence made Jake feel the heat on both sides, as if he were a slice of bread in a toaster.

Gloria's hazel eyes stared at him intently, daring him to confirm her obvious suspicions about why he was attending a prenatal appointment. Jenna cautiously took a half step back, trying to make sense of the situation.

"Well, I officially asked her out on our first date late last night. With all the other family drama yesterday, I didn't have the chance to tell you."

Gloria gave him a look that would freeze water, then jumped in with the gusto Jake had come to expect from her. "It sounds like you have a lot of explaining to do, Daddy."

"Daddy?" Jenna repeated, then laughed. "You mean Uncle."

Gloria rested the clipboard on her hip. "Hmm?"

"Jenna's my sister, Gloria. I'm here because her husband is away on a business trip. And because I learned from some great people recently what it means to support your family."

Jake could hear Gloria's breath as she finally exhaled fully.

"*Bien*." She looked at Jake and let a smile slip across her usually measured countenance. "Now come on back and let's take this baby's first photograph."

Jake stayed in the hallway while Gloria did the routine exam on Jenna. When the checkup was finished, she opened the door a crack. "Well, Uncle Jake? Are you ready to come in?"

Gloria bunched Jenna's loose blouse up and tucked in the elastic waistband of her new maternity pants, exposing the tiniest of baby bumps in her lower abdominal area. A computer sat on a stand next to where Jenna lay. Jake assumed that the ultrasound images would be shown on the flat-panel monitor perched on top.

"Are you ready?" Gloria asked Jenna with a warm smile.

Jenna nodded in reply. "Mm-hmm. It's still hard to believe this is all real."

"I do this every day, Jenna, and it never gets old. It's such a privilege to be able to see one of God's creations for the first time, and a few months later, help bring them into the world."

Gloria flipped a switch and then mouse-clicked her way through a few menus on the screen. The dim lighting in the room made Jake feel as if he was in some kind of sacred place.

And then he thought about Gloria's words and realized that, in a way, he was.

"Gloria, how did you come to be a midwife?" Jake asked with honest curiosity.

She grabbed a clear bottle filled with blue goop and squeezed it around Jenna's belly. "Honestly, Jake, it's all I've ever wanted to do—since I was a kid. Where Gracie and I come from, there's more of a tradition of midwifery. Especially in the small towns and rural areas."

She moved a small white probe around in little circles and the sound of whoosh-whoosh-whoosh came clearly through the speakers.

Awe struck Jake with a force that made him catch his breath. He could hear the heartbeat of his niece or nephew. It sounded strong. It sounded perfect. It sounded like the rarest of gifts. Jake knew he could never thank Jenna enough for asking him to join her for this moment.

Maybe he'd been wrong all along. Maybe his family did have a lot in common with Gracie's. Just because his parents weren't the kind of parents he'd often wished for didn't mean that the links of love didn't stretch over generations. Already, Jake knew he would do anything for this little creature growing inside Jenna. And Jenna herself. He had a family to be thankful for. This baby had just taught him a very important lesson.

No wonder God chose the same kind of miracle to teach all of humankind.

"So, you never wanted to work in a hospital?" Jenna asked as Gloria took measurements of the baby's head, arms, and legs with repetitive click sounds.

Gloria took her hand off the mouse. "Well, I used to work on the Labor and Delivery floor next door at Provident Medical Center. But after I lost my son and my husband, I had a hard time returning to the hospital. So, I started working here."

Gloria's last name was Rodriguez, not Garcia, so Jake knew she had been married. He'd noticed last night at Huarache's that she wasn't wearing a ring. But he just assumed she had probably gotten divorced. Or maybe she just didn't want masa dough squishing around a diamond.

But he'd never guessed that Gloria had lost her husband. And a child.

No wonder she was so protective of the family members she still had, like Gracie.

"I'm so glad you've been pointing out what everything is up there. I know the round part is the head, but the rest is like Greek to me." Jenna wiggled a little closer to the screen for a better look, then giggled, still staring intently at her baby on the screen.

Gloria punched a few more buttons. "I'll print out the screenshots I've been taking. There are about seven or eight of them. You can take them, so your husband can see baby's first pictures when he gets home."

Jenna beamed. Jake couldn't deny the truth of the old cliché. Pregnant women really did glow.

"Hey, Gloria, can I have a copy, too?" Like Jenna, Jake couldn't keep the smile off his face. "I want to be able to show off the newest member of my family."

Gloria handed a small, shiny square of paper to Jake. He stared at it and began to memorize the features of this tiny little person.

Just twenty-four hours ago, Jake felt his world being pulled out from under him, like sand displaced by a wave. But in this moment, with his sister and Gracie's sister—and the next generation—Jake felt renewed. Like his niece or nephew, he had the opportunity to grow and develop and pursue his dreams, whatever they wound up being.

He buried the old Jake, the son who was never good enough. The new Jake had his whole life ahead of him.

IN SPITE OF THE RAIN, Gracie slept all night long...and then she overslept.

But even though she was running late, she lay in bed a few minutes more than necessary, stretching. Gracie enjoyed the feeling of refreshment. The grass and trees received what they needed from the heavens last night in the form of rain. She received what she needed from Heaven last night in the form of a reprieve for El Centro.

And Jake's words to her, too. Dating David had left her so unsure of herself. His words and actions had made her self-conscious about who she was and where she'd come from.

She'd met David on her first day as a student at Provident College, when he conducted one of the orientation sessions she attended. She asked a question at the end of the class, and they found themselves talking about aspects of college life.

He'd been so easy to talk to at first. As a graduate student who then got a job in academic advisement at Provident

College, he'd initially been so supportive of her education. But then, as it became clear to her that her life's work would involve ESL education, he began to change. David told her she was wasting her time, that she'd need to choose a field that would garner more respect from others.

He said he had a reputation to uphold and she couldn't spend her time with "blue-collar people" if she was serious about a relationship with him because he was committed to moving up in his career of collegiate administration, where they would be surrounded by those with advanced educations. As he became more verbally abusive, Gracie found the only way to make a clean break from the relationship was to leave Provident College.

She started *El Centro* with no degree or much formal training, just a desire to help and mentor others. And even though she'd heard through the grapevine that David had left Port Provident last year for greener pastures, she still felt that scar on her heart and her self-worth every time she thought about returning to the classroom to complete her own degree—if she ever had the funds to again do so.

She'd assumed that since David's background was more similar to that of Jake's than her own, that Jake would hold the same opinions as the people who made up his world. Certainly, his initial desire to shut down her school did nothing but bolster that theory.

Of course, Gracie now knew Jake was different than she'd initially assumed. Jake's pedigree wasn't quite as advertised and she'd learned that he managed a bankruptcy judgment instead of a trust fund.

But last night, Gracie looked straight into Jake's heart. Titles and money didn't matter. A person with a caring heart and a newfound trust in God could become anything. Today marked the first day of that life for Jake, and Gracie felt so privileged to be a part of it.

She threw her feet over the side of the bed and rose, not wanting to waste another minute of this precious day. She showered quickly and got dressed, then went downstairs to begin setting up for the day's lessons. A full schedule of classes always filled her Saturdays. And on this particular Saturday, she knew thoughts of Jake would fill her mind.

"Miss Gracie?" Juan Calderon stuck his head in the classroom as Gracie pulled workbooks off the bookshelf. "Have you talked to Mr. Jake? My boss said he got fired yesterday afternoon. He was good for the company. I don't want it to be true."

The anxiety written across Juan's face touched Gracie. Jake once told her he wanted to change the bitter corporate culture his own father had built at Peoples Property Group. Juan's concern showed that even in his short tenure, Jake had made a difference in that regard.

"It is, Juan. The board of directors did not confirm him as CEO." Out of respect for Jake, Gracie left it there. God didn't want her to gossip, and she didn't, either. Too many other wagging tongues in a small town would take care of that soon enough.

"That's not good news, Gracie." Juan cast a glance at his brown boots, scuffed by the hard work of supervising landscape crews.

"No, not for Jake, it isn't. But there is a silver lining. *El Centro* won't be closing now, since they won't be expanding the condo project."

Juan looked up and smiled. "So, you'll still be teaching, Miss Gracie?"

"Absolutely. I'll be here for you, Juan, and all the other students." She carefully laid out the workbooks for those students.

"I'm going to go outside and wait for Pablo before class starts. He was wondering about Mr. Jake, too."

Juan ducked back out of the classroom and Gracie heard the front door quickly open and shut. Before she knew it, the room had filled up. Saturday morning's class was a favorite of Gracie's to teach. The men and women who came had been with Gracie for several years and were her most advanced group. They wanted to own their own businesses—students after Gracie's own heart.

"This is the last class before summer vacation, Gracie. What will we be covering today?" Carolina Sanchez pulled a spiral notebook from her white canvas bag. The corners of the blue cover frayed from use.

Gracie rolled the boxy black overhead projector on its wobbly metal cart to the front of the room. "Business plan basics. It'll be great for all of you to have something to work on during the break."

"Do you have room for one more?" A familiar voice came from just outside the door. Jake occupied her thoughts all morning, but she never imagined she'd see him before their date tonight.

She turned and answered him simply with a smile.

"Since today is our last class before we take a little summer vacation, I thought we would cover the basics of writing a business plan. When we get back together next month, I'll expect you to have completed plans for the businesses you hope to open." She picked the first slide up off the top of the stack but didn't lay it on the projector's glass just yet. "Class, we have a guest today who can provide some great insight."

She gestured at the man who took her breath away every time she stole a glance in his direction. "Jake Peoples has a master of business administration degree from the University of Texas and another degree from the university's law school."

He shook his head like a dog after a run through a sprinkler. "No, Gracie, I don't think so."

Gracie often brought in guest speakers to share their expertise with her advanced classes, but never before had someone with Jake's background been in the audience. It seemed so logical to her that he would share his knowledge with this small and striving group.

"Why not?"

"I think you know why." The words gritted out through Jake's clenched jaw. His eyes took on the same mossy shade as the night before when he'd revealed the unexpected outcome of the board meeting.

She'd meant her words for praise, but Jake heard condemnation. Every time he'd tried to lead a business—first his law firm, then his short stint as CEO of Peoples Property Group—it had not ended well. Gracie didn't want to add to Jake's burden. If anything, she wanted to take it away.

He may not have found the right way to showcase his talent yet, but Gracie knew Jake was a smart man who genuinely cared about the people he served in business. If anything, Jake cared too much. And it was hard to fault someone who cared too much. As far as *El Centro* was concerned, Gracie knew she was guilty of the same thing. Why else had she panicked when faced with the Maximized Revenue Zones? If serving her students hadn't been at the top of her priority list, she wouldn't have spent every waking hour of the last week trying to think of one way after another to save her school.

Well, every waking hour she wasn't thinking of Jake.

"I understand, Jake. But feel free to chime in whenever you feel like it. I really think the class would benefit from what you've learned over the years." She laid another slide up on the projector, wishing she could make her heart's desire as clear to Jake as the neat rows of small black text on the illuminated screen. "These are tips from the Small Business Administration. You'll need to put together a description of the business, gather your financial data and attach supporting documents, like your personal tax returns and your resume."

Jake raised his hand, like a courteous student. He spoke slowly, as though he'd thought hard before deciding to finally speak. "Gracie, I have some really good templates for balance sheets and cash flow and items like that. Maybe I could set something up for the folks who are interested in learning more."

Relief washed over Gracie. She hadn't completely alienated him with her earlier request. It made her smile to see the highly educated businessman reaching out to help others get a solid start. "That would be great, Jake, since we're almost out of time with today's class. Would anyone be interested in meeting one-on-one with Jake during the break to talk about numbers in greater depth?"

Every hand in the room shot up, then chatter in both Spanish and English filled the small room as the class ended.

"We'll still see you around, Mr. Jake. We'll both be here for your budget class." Pablo said on his way to the door.

"Good. I know you will both go on to do great things. You're both some of the hardest-working men I've ever met."

"Thanks, Mr. Jake." Juan nodded with a shy pride at the compliment. "Maybe we'll see you at church again soon."

Jake winked at Gracie. "I think you'll see me tomorrow."

"I think so, too." Gracie grinned.

El Centro would remain open and she now had a wonderful man who wanted to be part of all the aspects of her life—family, church, school. Everything seemed to be falling into place.

Juan and Pablo said their goodbyes, and Gracie and Jake stood alone in the classroom. "I didn't mean to single you out," she said.

"I know you didn't. That's why I said I'd come back and help out. At the least, Johnny Peoples paid for me to get a very good education. I haven't been able to use it in the ways I thought I would, but as I listened to you teach, I realized that's no reason I can't share the things I know with others."

Jake clasped both her hands in his. She warmed at the simple touch.

"And now, Gracie Garcia, I want to share the rest of my day with you. Are you ready?"

She laughed at his mischievous grin. "Ready for what?"

"A genuine, official date. Go upstairs and grab your bathing suit and some sunscreen and some rubber soled shoes."

"Rubber-soled shoes?" Her mind rolled in somersaults. "What on earth do you have planned?"

"Freedom."

WITH GRACIE BY HIS side in the passenger seat, Jake pulled the truck underneath an arch reading "Port Provident Boat Club."

Gracie looked one way and back the other, taking it all in.

"Have you ever been here before?"

She shook her head. "No, I haven't."

"Good, mission number one accomplished. I'm bringing you someplace new." He pulled into a parking space and stopped the car. "Okay, stay right there."

He ran past the tailgate and came around to open her door. Jake knew he wasn't Prince Charming— illegitimate sons never got the keys to the kingdom, as he'd painfully learned this week—but he could still see to it that Gracie was treated like a princess today.

"Madame." He bowed with a flourish worthy of becoming the fourth Musketeer.

Gracie playfully slapped him on the head and laughed. "What are you doing?"

"I'm taking you out on the water for the afternoon." Jake reached behind the passenger seat and grabbed the canvas bag he'd made Gracie pack before they left her house.

He held her hand as they walked down a small pier connecting the floating marina to the parking lot. Their footsteps echoed loudly on the wooden planks as they turned down a narrow passageway covered by an industrial-looking metal roof. Boat slips jutted out on either side as far as the eye could see.

"You have a boat?" Gracie stepped cautiously.

"No. I just happen to know people who do." He guided her around a puddle of water on the walkway. "Bankruptcy court would never have allowed me to keep such a luxury."

Jake stopped three slips before the end of the row. "Here we are."

The boat was a beauty. White hull, blue stripes. It had a cobalt-blue bimini top covering most of the back half of the boat. Named *The Getaway Girl*, it wasn't the fanciest boat at the Port Provident Boat Club, and the size fell solidly in the midrange of the others moored around it, but it did have a small room and a bathroom down a short flight of stairs located just behind the elevated console.

"Your chariot, Madame." Jake gave another exaggerated bow, then rose and extended his hand.

Gracie reached for it without taking her eyes off the floating beauty in front of her. Chips, sodas and cookies lay arranged under a wire mesh tent atop the small table in the back seating area. A vase filled with two dozen roses of every color—pink, yellow, white and red—sat primly in a short vase wedged securely into a cupholder on the table's corner.

"How did you do all this?" she said as he helped guide her up the small step ladder and onto the deck.

"Well," Jake said, climbing onboard, "let's just say you're not the only one with an awesome sister. This boat belongs to

Jenna and her husband. Mitch likes to take it out for overnight fishing trips on weekends. But he's out of town today."

"I've never been on anything like this before, Jake."

"What do you mean?" He crossed to the side of the boat and released the moorings. Walking quickly around the vessel's perimeter, Jake made sure everything was ready to go, even though he knew Jenna had just set up the surprise and would have left *The Getaway Girl* seaworthy.

"We used to own a little aluminum boat when I was a girl. Papí would take it out fishing, but it didn't even have padding on the seats. This is amazing."

"Not as amazing as the woman I get to spend the afternoon with." Jake climbed up to the console and took a seat behind the wheel. "Come on up. Let's go. You can be my first mate."

He watched her walk toward him, her hair pulled back in a ponytail and her delicate face shaded by a hot pink sun visor. A floral-printed bow on her bathing suit was tied around her neck, and she wore a loose cotton cover-up. Gracie might be stunned by the boat, but Jake felt in awe of her.

He'd bestowed the title of first mate on her for the afternoon but had to beat out of his head the thought of her becoming his true first mate for life. A woman like Gracie—strong, determined, full of faith and spirit— didn't deserve a man like him—a man who so far had only demonstrated he couldn't make a success out of anything he tried to do.

Except today. He would be successful at making her smile today.

Jake turned the ignition and the boat rumbled to life. Gracie wrapped her fingers around the edge of the seat. "Are you ready, First Mate Garcia?"

"Aye aye, *el capitán.*"

After an afternoon of cruising around Provident Bay, Jake decided to drop anchor. A few orange streaks began to gather in the sky. The sun would be setting soon. He had one more surprise planned.

"Why don't you go back to the table and grab us each another soda out of the cooler? I'm going to run downstairs for a second."

Taking the stairs two by two, Jake didn't waste any time. He found the box his sister had carefully set in the boat's tiny kitchen. He opened the refrigerator and pulled out the last few items he needed and ran back upstairs with the box.

"Gracie?"

"Up here."

She turned around and waved at him from the bow of the vessel. The setting sun lit her normally dark hair with highlights, turning it the shade of molten copper. Barefoot, in a halter-top bikini and matching board shorts, Gracie seemed as though she'd been on the water her whole life.

"You look beautiful." The words sounded too simple to describe the true picture she painted.

The corner of her mouth twisted in a half smile. "Thanks."

"You do. I know you said you haven't heard that in a while, but you need to be told that every day— because it's true. Especially right now."

He wanted to make her understand just how much he meant the words, but holding the box interfered with the moment. So, he set it down on the ground and went about executing the rest of his plan.

He had to get this right. One tablecloth, spread out across the deck. Two of those new flameless candles he'd seen advertised on TV. Two of his sister's best crystal stemware pieces. One giant bottle of sparkling water and a lemon twist for each glass. Two plates from his sister's wedding china, along with a pair of matching fabric napkins snug inside pearl-encrusted napkin rings.

He set everything carefully on the heavy silk cloth, challenged somewhat by the constant soft bobbing of the boat on the water.

"What are you doing?" Gracie walked over and knelt beside him.

"Dinner." Jake smiled. In the middle of the bay, it was difficult to pull off a fancy dinner, so he hoped the atmosphere and the china made up for the main course. "BLT submarine sandwiches and potato chips. Nothing but the best for my crew."

She laughed, then stopped. "I couldn't have asked for more. This is amazing."

"Well, there's more." Jake reached in once more and pulled out a plastic container. A dozen green stems peeked above juicy red luxury. "Chocolate-dipped strawberries for dessert. Jenna made them herself. Actually, she made all the food."

Jake carefully poured the bubbly water into each champagne flute. "A toast."

Gracie raised her glass.

"To a woman whose faith that all things are possible made an unbearable few days bearable." He clinked his glass lightly against the side of Gracie's. "Thank you for being there for me. Thank you for being you."

"Oh, Jake."

The calm in Jake's heart turned to a little bit of panic at the pause in her words. What was she trying to gather her thoughts to say?

"Thank you for bringing me out and arranging this wonderful day. No one's ever gone to this much trouble for me. When I first met you, I didn't think I could really trust you. I thought you were going to crush all my dreams for my school and never even give a second thought to the damage you were causing. I misjudged you."

Gracie and Jake talked some about that first meeting—not even a week ago—and companionably ate the dinner Jenna had prepared. In typical Jenna fashion, the BLTs were clearly made with love. She'd built each sandwich on fluffy French loaves, spread them with pesto and garnished both with fresh mozzarella cheese. They weren't ordinary BLT sandwiches, and this was no ordinary evening.

Waves lapped against the side of the boat and their sweet sound fit the moment more perfectly than any symphony. "I don't know what I'm going to do next, Gracie. Too many of my dreams have been lost this last year. I placed my trust in a client who lied to me and cost me my business and more. I tried to earn back the trust of the board of directors at my family's company, only to find out I couldn't give them the only thing that mattered to them—DNA—and I didn't even know it."

Jake paused, looking around, and then focusing back on Gracie with intensity. "I don't think I told you that I'm going to be an uncle—Jenna's expecting—and the more I think about what having another generation means in my life, the more I want to make sure I get things right. I went with Jenna to her prenatal checkup today—she's a patient of Gloria's, believe it or not—and I got to hear the heartbeat of the next member of my family. Then I came to your school and talked with your students. It's all made me realize I enjoy connecting with people the most. I may not have been the most successful attorney during my time in Austin, but I allowed myself to believe my client's false story simply because I wanted to help others. I still do."

Gracie wiped her hands after finishing her last bite of BLT. "I know you'll find something that suits you. Maybe you could teach business classes at the college? I had to leave my studies there because of...personal reasons...but I've always hoped I could finish my teaching degree so I can continue to help others."

"I have to find a job sooner rather than later. I do have a settlement I have to pay as part of the bankruptcy." He paused. "Seeing the enthusiasm of your students today made me realize that whatever I do, I need to do something that touches individual lives."

Her smile gave him strength as he began turning this new corner in life. "Are you ready to pull up anchor? I want to head back for the marina before it gets dark. If anything happens to the boat, Mitch might not forgive me. And I'll be picking you up bright and early for church tomorrow."

"Yes. Let's get everything cleaned up." Gracie shook the bread and chip crumbs from both plates overboard. Not much else was left—they'd eaten every scrumptious bite. Carefully, she laid the delicate plates and glasses back in the box.

A few minutes later, Jake joined Gracie at the bow. She stood silently, taking one last look at the splashes of orange and yellow in the sky. Jake slipped an arm around her waist, grateful for the moment.

He turned and looked Gracie in the eye. Her gaze reminded him of a chocolate lava cake he'd once had at a fancy restaurant—sweetness on the outside and warm pudding on the inside.

It was a wordless moment, and she seemed to be searching him as much as he was searching her. He knew what he was looking for—and needed to know if she felt the same way.

Carefully, he pulled her close.

Suddenly, he could no longer see the chocolate in her eyes, but could taste the sweetness in her kiss. She didn't pull back and Jake made the moment last a little longer, enjoying the feel of the breeze, the sway of the water and the tenderness of the woman in his arms. He felt stirred to the soul.

When the kiss ended, they stood in a companionable silence, Gracie's head resting on Jake's shoulder as they gazed at the sky with its deep gold and orange streaks that cut through the clouds and shimmered on the water.

He couldn't feel much certainty in his life right now, but he knew he'd never question or regret this moment.

Gracie turned toward Jake and broke the silence. "Did you ever hear back from Councilman Porter?"

He couldn't decide if the burnished sky or her copper highlights shone with more fire. "No, I didn't. But I told him not to call unless there was a problem. So, it looks like everything's taken care of for Monday's meeting."

"Good. That's the icing on the cake of a perfect weekend." She smiled with a brightness that put the setting sun to shame.

"And the weekend's not over yet."

"What do you mean?" Gracie looked at him with genuine interest. It felt good to know she didn't want the moment to end, either.

"Have you ever been to Summer Street Fest downtown? It's tonight."

Gracie shook her head. "No, I haven't. Usually when there's a festival like that in town, the crowds at Huarache's are pretty strong, so I wind up helping out with a couple of shifts at the restaurant."

As Jake intertwined his fingers with Gracie's, he noticed that her hands—like everything else about her— were soft. He loved that Gracie wasn't jaded. She still saw the sparkle of sunshine in life.

"I haven't been there in years," Jake said. "But I can't think of anyone I'd rather go back with."

He squeezed her soft palm once, then twice. She returned the gesture and the electric frisson that shot through him caught Jake by surprise.

He couldn't deny it. He'd fallen for Gracie.

AFTER A FEW HOURS AT Summer Street Fest, eating ice cream and window shopping in all the stores downtown, Jake walked Gracie to her front door. "Sweet dreams. I'll see you in the morning. I'll be here about forty-five minutes before church starts so we'll have time to pick up doughnuts or a breakfast burrito on the way."

"That sounds great. Thank you for such a wonderful day, Jake. I'll never forget it."

She unlocked the door and stepped inside. He waited on the porch long enough to hear Gracie turn the lock and see the hall light come on.

Satisfied that she was safely inside, Jake climbed in the truck and turned toward home. One of his favorite songs, a Creedence Clearwater Revival classic, came on the radio. Jake rolled down the window and let the sea breeze blow through his hair.

His whole world had come crashing down during the last twenty-four hours, and yet he felt like celebrating.

Time with Gracie changed his whole outlook on life. The cell phone he'd casually tossed in the car's cupholder earlier started to ring. He almost didn't want to answer it because he was having so much fun singing.

But it might be Gracie and he didn't want to miss hearing her voice one more time tonight. "Hello?"

"Jake, it's Jenna." Her voice quivered.

"Everything went great today—thank you again for all the help. The boat's safe and sound. Don't be so worried."

He laughed at his sister panicking over her husband's pride and joy.

"I'm not calling about the boat, Jake. It's Nana. She's had a heart attack. You need to get to Provident Medical Center right now."

Chapter Ten

GRACIE FELT THANKFUL for hardwood flooring. She would have worn a hole in a carpet with the number of times in the last twenty minutes she'd walked to the small digital clock on her nightstand.

Jake should have arrived to pick her up almost half an hour ago. Church would start in less than ten minutes.

She picked up her cell phone and pressed two keys, triggering the redial function.

Ring.

Ring.

Ring.

"You've reached Jake Peoples. I can't take your call right now..."

Gracie hung up. She'd heard the automated message about ten times already. And she'd left three messages. Gracie didn't see the sense in leaving any more.

Nor did she see the sense in waiting any longer. She would miss worship by continuing to stall. Gracie grabbed her keys and purse off the table near her small bathroom and headed downstairs.

Maybe Jake had forgotten that he'd committed to picking her up. That explanation seemed plausible. He was probably already sitting at church, saving her a seat and sharing a laugh with Mamí and Papí.

In fact, they were probably all wondering why she was running so late. She needed to get her little blue Ford in gear and get on the road—without thinking of Jake, whose car repair help and borrowed screw a few days ago made it possible for her car to start this morning.

Outside the church, Gracie saw dozens of cars she recognized, but not the one gray truck she hoped for. Maybe Jake parked in the next block or around the back.

Mariela Ramos began to play a hymn's opening notes as Gracie opened the door to the sanctuary. Even though the song signaled the beginning of church, Gracie didn't rush to find a seat. She stayed put in the doorway, scanning the back of everyone's head looking for one particular short, dirty-blond haircut.

"Gracie!" Gloria's attempt at whispering could be heard by the crowd in the back half of the sanctuary. She waved her hand.

Gloria moved her Bible off the seat it had been saving and Gracie slid into her spot. She stayed perched on the edge of the seat, unable to settle in. She should have watched the choir singing, looked through her bulletin and located the day's verse in her Bible. She should have focused on God while she sat in His house.

But Gracie couldn't keep her eyes off the door.

Where was Jake?

"What's the matter?" Gloria passed Gracie a note scrawled across the top corner of the bulletin.

Gracie waved her hand dismissively and shook her head. "Nothing."

She pushed the trifold back to her sister. The speed at which Gloria's eyebrows shot up wordlessly told Gracie her sister wasn't going to leave it at that. She knew there was something behind the quick denial. Gloria picked up her pen again, but Mamí plucked it from her fingers. They'd never been allowed to pass notes in church, and even though they were both grown, Mamí's rules remained steadfast.

The choir started singing one of Gracie's favorite hymns. She tried to listen to the voices raised in praise. But the doubt in her head drowned out all the surrounding sounds of grace.

Pastor Ruiz stepped to the pulpit. "*Bienvenidos, mi familia.* Today we're going to speak about a topic affecting us all. Trust. Worrying. What does Jesus say about these two things? In Matthew 6:34, He says plainly 'Therefore, do not worry about tomorrow, for tomorrow will worry about itself. Each day has enough trouble of its own.'"

Oh, boy, did it. The words hit home to Gracie. But instead of focusing on the preacher's lesson, she found herself drawn into her own worries, rehashing them in her mind.

An hour later, Gracie still couldn't control her mental wanderlust.

"Yoo-hoo? Where have you been all morning?" Gloria poked at Gracie's shoulder for emphasis. Gracie kept walking, winding her way through the small after-church crowd in the foyer.

"Hmm?"

"Exactly. You've just proven my point. What is on your mind?" Gloria stopped Gracie from exiting the church. "Is it Jake?"

Gracie blinked, trying to clear the fog from her mind. "*Qué*?"

"Jake. The guy you've thought about all the time recently."

"He's not here." She tried to scan the faces nearby. Maybe she just missed seeing him in the sanctuary.

"I know he's not and, mentally, neither are you. What is going on?" Gloria took Gracie by the chin and turned her face, bringing them eye-to-eye.

"He said he'd pick me up for church this morning, but he didn't show."

Gloria dropped her hand. "When did he tell you he was coming?"

"Last night, after our date." She let out a breath she hadn't realized she'd been holding. Gracie could feel the pins and needles she'd sat on all morning. As the numbness wore off, the hurt began to set in. "He said he'd be back in the morning for church, then he went to give the boat keys back to his sister."

"Jenna Peoples Carson? That sister?" A spark of animation popped into Gloria's voice.

"Yes, why?"

Gloria only sounded like this when her instinct kicked in, and Gracie knew from experience not to discount Gloria's gut feelings. Her sister frowned, which didn't reassure Gracie about what was coming next.

"Jenna Carson is a patient of mine. In fact, Jake was with her at yesterday's appointment and I thought he was there as the father, not the uncle. So I made it clear I was his girlfriend's sister. She was surprised to hear he even had a girlfriend. She seems very nice, but Jenna Carson is the number two person in charge of the largest foundation in town. She sits on the board of every major charity on this island and her face is pictured on the society page every single week. What if she said something about his new girlfriend after they left the clinic yesterday?"

Gracie took a step back. That didn't sound at all like the sister Jake described. Jenna had even set up the boat and made that delicious meal for Jake and Gracie. But the pins and needles poked more, leaving a burning sensation. Maybe Gloria was onto something.

"What are you getting at?" "They're already in the middle of a huge storm because of the revelations at the board meeting. The Peoples name is damaged goods right now. If it got out that Jake was dating a girl like you, there would be even more fires to put out."

Gloria's words drove into Gracie like a punch to the gut. A blow in a boxing ring would have inflicted less pain than the shot to Gracie's pride, to the heart of her insecurities.

"A girl like me?" She desperately hoped her sister meant something other than the way Gracie took the comment.

Gloria nodded. "An immigrant from Mexico. You do good work at your school. I help women—even those like Jenna Carson—bring new life into the world. But this is a small town, and you and I both know none of that matters to certain groups of people."

Gracie knew Gloria wasn't pulling a wild theory out of thin air. She remembered everything—and she never would have forgotten how David treated her kid sister years ago.

How could Gracie have been so blind not to see the reality again? How could she be so naive? Jake might have expressed feelings for her yesterday, but it wouldn't take long for him to be set straight about the reality of trying to rebuild his reputation while in a relationship with a girl from the other side of town.

"Do you really believe that, Gloria?" The words came out in a whisper. Each syllable scraped her throat raw.

Her older sister answered without a blink or a flinch. "Of course I do."

The cell phone vibrated in the truck's cupholder where it lay, forgotten in the frenzy of the past twenty-four hours. After four rings, the voice-mail message came on in lieu of the owner's personal greeting.

"You've reached Jake Peoples. I can't take your call right now. Please leave your name, number, and a brief message. I'll return your call as soon as possible. Thanks."

Beep.

"Jake. It's Carter Porter. I just got your message—I've been out of town with the family. Look, I can't take back the proposal. We have to move forward. You're not the only one who was interested in the Maximized Revenue Zones. I'll see you at the meeting tomorrow and we'll discuss it more. Bye."

GRACIE'S HEART SKIPPED a beat as she pushed open the heavy door to the City Council's chambers. She hadn't planned on coming to the meeting since Jake told her he'd decided to call off the proposal. But she hadn't heard from him all day yesterday and after a sleepless night, she needed to talk to him—needed to know Gloria's theory was wrong—and she was running out of logical places to get answers.

She even made a midnight drive past his grandmother's estate. The familiar truck wasn't parked out front, and she couldn't see a single light on, either in the carriage house or the main house.

Gracie didn't know why he wasn't answering his phone or where he'd gone. But maybe he'd be at the meeting today. It was her best hope of finding him and asking the questions drilling a hole in her brain.

The more Gracie thought about it, the more Gloria's statement after church made too much sense.

Just like yesterday at church, though, Gracie didn't see Jake in the crowd. She took a seat near the back so she could watch for him, unnoticed by the rest of those gathered to hear Port Provident's official business.

At least she only needed to worry about finding Jake, not about saving El Centro. If she hadn't been told that the outcome of this meeting was secure, she didn't think she'd be able to handle it.

Thank goodness she knew Jake had left the message for Carter Porter and that Jake told her yesterday things appeared to be straightened out. Gracie really only wanted to deal with one major source of stress at a time.

"All right, everyone, let's call today's meeting to order." Mayor Blankenship spoke into the microphone placed in front of her. "Let the record show that we have a quorum. First on the agenda today, we will revisit the issue of Maximized Revenue Zones on Gulfview Boulevard. Councilman Porter, the floor is yours."

A little kick of adrenaline surged into Gracie's bloodstream. Shouldn't something else be on the agenda?

But Jake said things were going to be okay. She clung to the reassurance he'd given her, even if nothing else about Jake made sense right now. She assumed Jake's friend would set the record straight and then her heart rate could slow back to normal.

"Thank you, Madam Mayor. We held off the vote last week to give businesses affected by the proposal the opportunity to get their affairs in order. Now that we've done our due diligence for our business owners in that matter, I'd like to propose that we move immediately to a vote on the proposal without any further discussion. Do I have a second?"

A vote? A second?

Suddenly, the weight of her deepest fears pushed on Gracie's lungs. She couldn't breathe. Wordlessly, her mouth opened and shut, then opened again.

Councilman Ben Gartner looked at his colleague and nodded. "Second."

With an involuntary gasp, respiration kicked back in. But the rapid shallow inhalations and exhalations made Gracie light-headed in seconds. She gripped the sides of the chair until the pads of her fingers tingled with pain in order to keep from falling over.

"Let's vote, then." The mayor wasted no time in moving things along. "Regarding the proposal for Maximized Revenue Zones on Gulfview Boulevard, let all those in favor raise their hand and say 'aye.'"

Four hands went up, including the mayor's. An affirmative chorus pierced Gracie's eardrums.

Everything happened so quickly. Gracie couldn't keep up with the speed of the City Council as they approved the ordinance.

"We have four votes in favor. All those against raise your hand and say 'nay.'"

Only Angela Ruiz's hand rose in dissent.

The gavel came down with a crack. It sounded like the breaking of Gracie's heart.

"Let the record show that the proposal for Maximized Revenue Zones on Gulfview Boulevard has passed, four-to-one. All affected parties will be notified this week and the new ordinance will be effective at the first of the coming month." The mayor laid the small mallet back in the cradle at the edge of the table. "Next up, Councilman Gartner has requested that we discuss a change in the water rate."

Just like the final buzzer sounding at a championship game, the battle came to an end. Gracie's world changed with lightning speed.

One day before, she'd been secure in her work and her relationships. Now, she didn't have a school and she couldn't find Jake.

Jake.

Is this what he'd felt like Friday when he lost his job and his family heritage?

Jake.

The same person who told her El Centro would be okay. The same person who cared for her.

She'd spent so long building her walls back up after David's disregard for her feelings and her school. Gracie had repaired her broken heart and wounded trust by promising herself she'd remain self-sufficient. That she'd take care of El Centro and herself by herself.

And then, in a short period, she'd allowed Jake Peoples and his fancy law school talk to make her forget every hard lesson she'd ever learned.

She almost couldn't forgive herself for her own stupidity. How could she have trusted him?

She couldn't think about Jake now. She couldn't think about anything. Whirring at blazing speed just moments before, her mind now cooled into a numb crawl.

The City Council members began their next debate, but Gracie couldn't hear another word through her frozen haze. She rose unsteadily, not caring about protocol. She knew she shouldn't just walk out of the meeting like this, but Gloria was right. No one in this room would care what someone who came from the wrong side of the border did anyway.

Pushing the solid door open took every ounce of Gracie's remaining strength. Her footfalls across the marble foyer sounded to her ears like echoes in a mausoleum. Truthfully, that's what City Hall just became to her. The place that housed the death of her dreams.

All of them. Her school, which she'd built from nothing. And Jake, for whom she'd let down her guard. She'd been so wrong to waste her time on both. She didn't have anything to show for either effort.

Until this minute, Gracie had believed with all her heart in faith and hard work. God answered all her recent prayers with a clear "no."

That broke her heart more than anything.

She'd been so wrong about it all.

Gracie reached out for a nearby wall to steady herself. She leaned back, wanting to take a few moments to compose herself. Instead, her knees buckled and she slowly slid down the length of the cold green stone. She reached the floor and pulled up her knees, then rested her head, too exhausted by the battle to fight anymore.

THE NURSE'S SHOES SQUEAKED on the linoleum outside the door to the room in the ICU. Jake hadn't left Nana's side since arriving at the hospital more than twenty-four hours ago. He needed a shower and a shave.

More than that, he needed to apologize for his words the other night. He couldn't bear the thought that those might be the last words he ever got to say to Nana.

Jake squirmed a little in the chair. Whoever bought furniture for Provident Medical Center clearly put cost before comfort. The thin cushions were covered in a burnt-orange vinyl that squeaked when anyone sat down. He rolled his shoulders back and around once, twice, three times. Anything to get comfortable.

Jenna touched Jake's shoulder, shaking him from his thoughts. "Jake, we have to talk." Her usually sparkly voice sounded flat.

"I know, Jenna. The doctor said we may have to make some decisions soon. I've just been hoping it wouldn't come to that. Do you think we're there?"

She nodded. "We may be close. And before we get there, we have to decide what to do with the foundation."

The Peoples Family Foundation easily rated as the last thing on Jake's mind. "What do you mean?"

"Well, I turned in my resignation after I found out I was expecting. My last day is next Friday. With my history of hypoglycemia, Gloria felt that it would be best if I eliminated as much stress from my life as possible for the next few months. And Mitch and I have always wanted me to be a stay-at-home mom."

Between the revelations about her brother and Nana's stay in the ICU, Jake knew that the last few days had been anything but stress-free. "Okay. I understand."

"But even if Nana...comes back to us...she can't keep up with the demands of the foundation and being on the board at the company."

Jake could hear Jenna forcing words around the lump in her throat. He recognized the sound because he'd been battling the same stone hardness ever since he got that fateful phone call.

"You're right, Jenna." Jake nodded in agreement. "But I'm starving and I can't think straight. Let me run down to the cafeteria and get a candy bar or something and I'll come back and we can talk it through. Do you want anything?"

"No. I'm fine for now. All I want is for things to be the way they used to be." She turned her gaze back to Nana and her soft words got lost in the steady beeping of the machines monitoring Diana Peoples's vital signs.

"I know." He blew a kiss to his sleeping grandmother on the narrow hospital bed. "Be right back."

He couldn't look at Nana under the blanket of wires and tubes for long. It reminded Jake that the doctors considered her prognosis touch-and-go.

Even the strongest of hearts could wear out.

Jake walked down the long, fluorescent-illuminated hallway, alone with his thoughts. What would become of him without Nana—especially now that the secret about his heritage had come out? How would he rebuild his life without the foundation on which he'd always relied? He didn't see how he could help Jenna with the burdens on her shoulders now that it was revealed that he was a Peoples in name only.

As he rounded the corner to the cafeteria, his train of thought drifted, and Gracie came to his mind. The image seemed so clear—almost as if she was standing in front of him.

"Jake?" The voice cut into his thoughts. "You need to get out of here before she sees you."

"What?" He did a double take. Gloria Garcia Rodriguez blocked his path to the vending machine. She narrowed her eyes and gritted her jaw.

"Gracie. After what you did to her..." She paused, then launched in again. "You need to leave."

"Gloria, I don't understand." He looked over Gloria's petite frame and saw Gracie near the soda fountain. "What are you doing here?"

"I work next door, remember? One of my clients had complications in labor and had to be admitted here. I'm bringing lunch to the family. Gracie's with me. She needed a shoulder to cry on today."

Gloria looked him up, then down. The searing anger in her gaze locked on Jake like a missile that had found its target. "No thanks to you."

What? Gloria kept talking in blame-filled riddles. Clearly he wasn't going to get answers from her. He needed to make his way to Gracie and ask her personally.

If he could get her pit bull of a sister to let him through.

She dogged each step he tried to take.

"Let me pass, Gloria."

"No." One determined syllable said it all. Only one tactic remained for him to try.

"Gracie!" At his shout, every cafeteria patron's head snapped around and stared straight at him. He took a quick step and edged past Gloria.

As he neared, Gracie put her hand out. He could see a sheen of tears across her chocolate brown eyes, clouding them. "No, Jake," she said softly.

"You've got to tell me what's wrong. Why is Gloria giving me the evil eye?"

Gracie looked down at the floor, then up at Jake. She stuck a fingernail in her mouth and bit down before speaking softly through clenched teeth. "Because you lied to me."

"I did what?" Jake began to doubt his ears. First, he couldn't believe his entire family hid the truth of his parentage from him his whole life. Then, he couldn't believe Nana's life was in jeopardy. And now, he couldn't believe Gracie thought he'd been untruthful with her.

"I trusted you, Jake. You let me down. I've never really believed anyone when they said they wanted to be with me. I trusted you. You said you called Carter Porter and that I could keep my school." Tears squeezed out of her eyes, but she continued. "But you stood me up yesterday, just like every other man from your side of town has. You've figured out I'm not good enough for you. Then today that ordinance you said you'd stopped passed. Did you even really make that phone call? How could Carter Porter ask for a vote on your special proposal if you told him not to? Your actions closed *El Centro*. Everything was clearly a lie."

It all sounded like the teacher from the Charlie Brown specials, spoken with a bitter Spanish accent. None of her words made any sense.

"You're not good enough for me? What do you mean, Gracie?"

"Come on, Jake. You and your family can't afford any more scandal this week. Why else would you be afraid to be seen on the wrong side of the tracks with the wrong girl or to actually go to bat for her school?"

"Gracie, that's nonsense." The whole room could hear them arguing—some of them Nana's friends—but Jake didn't care. He needed to make this right. But how? He didn't understand, much less know where to start.

"No, it's not." She turned her face away. "I can't...I can't talk to you any more." She clapped her hand over her mouth and dropped her head, then turned and quickly made her way through the maze of tables.

Jake started to follow her, but Gracie's chief protector intercepted him. "Leave her alone," Gloria said in a tone that left no room for discussion. "You've done enough damage. She's been calling and calling for two days. Why won't you answer your phone?"

"I haven't gotten any calls." Jake reached in his pocket to prove his point, but it was empty. His stomach grew queasy. "Oh, no. I bet it's still in my car. I've been at the ICU with Nana since I left Gracie's house Saturday night. Nana had a heart attack. My whole world has been a haze of surgeries and consent forms and standing vigil with my sister."

Gloria gave him a wary look.

"Look at this chin if you don't believe me." Jake pulled his hand across two days' worth of stubble. "I haven't had a shower in forty-eight hours. I haven't been home, I haven't left Nana's room. These are the same clothes I was wearing when I left Gracie's house Saturday night. I don't know what she's talking about. Gloria, you have to help me."

A chime rang from the pocket on Gloria's scrubs. She pulled out her cell phone and looked at the screen. "I have a mother in early labor at the clinic. It looks like she needs me."

"But I need Gracie."

Gloria started to take a step and then stopped. "When you stood her up for church yesterday, I told her that I figured your family didn't want any more scandals this week and you didn't want to be seen with a girl from the wrong side of the tracks."

Jake shook his head.

Gloria kept talking. "Your friend on the City Council got the resolution passed. Gracie has to close her school. She's probably gone home to pack." She punched a button on the phone in her hand. "It's funny. People always look to money to solve problems. Your family has all the money in the world, but it doesn't seem to help. In our family, we never had money. We just had faith. Now Gracie thinks that's deserted her, too."

She slipped away quietly, leaving Jake by himself in the middle of the crowded cafeteria. He heard footsteps behind him and hoped to see Gracie, returning to listen, to let him explain the misunderstanding.

When he turned around, he saw his brother-in-law, Mitch.

"Jake, Jenna said I'd find you here. Nana's awake and she's asking for you."

Chapter Eleven

JAKE KNEW HE NEEDED to focus on Nana. But his concentration kept slipping.

He felt divided.

Jenna and Mitch left the room to catch some fresh air, leaving Jake and Nana alone, except for the constant company of the bank of monitors over the bed.

"We need to talk, Jakey." Nana's voice scratched like dry twigs in winter.

He patted her hand, thankful to hear her voice in any fashion again.

"About what?"

She took a long, deep breath. "Everything that's happened. We need to finish our conversation on why I've stayed silent all these years."

Jake's eyes widened. Forty-eight hours in a coma, and her relationship with her not-quite-grandson was the first thing on her mind?

"But you knew from the beginning."

"Of course I did, dear boy." Her squeeze felt like the flutter of butterfly wings. "But it didn't matter to me. I've loved you since the moment you were born, just two floors above where we are now. I knew your mother was a flirt and a social climber. She and your father were alike in that way. It always pained me that your father acted that way, as if his name and his money made him special. Your grandfather thought we needed to send him to that fancy boarding school in the Northeast. I still wonder if I'd fought harder and kept him home, would he have turned out differently?"

Jake couldn't remember his grandmother speaking so frankly before. "You're not usually the type to talk about regrets, Nana."

"Well, Jakey, I'm not the type to think about dying, either, but you do a lot of that when you're lying in a hospital bed." The corners of her mouth turned up, warming her whole face. "I knew the secret about you, but I'd forgotten about the bylaws. I wouldn't have ever set you up in that manner. I hope you know that."

A lump formed in Jake's throat. Nana's inherent nature was too good to concoct such a scheme, but he couldn't find the words to let her know he forgave her completely. Another pat on the hand would have to suffice.

"I'll never regret having a reason to bring you home, Jakey. This year's been rough for you, losing your father and your law practice. I wanted to make your road a little easier. I didn't plan on things going this way. But I'm not a quitter, and blood relative or not, I helped raise you and I know you have my fighting spirit. This isn't the end for you with the Peoples family or Port Provident."

Jake let go of Nana's hand and walked to the window. He stared blankly at the street below. "But I don't see how to overcome this one, Nana. And now I've lost Gracie, too."

"Gracie? Who is that?" Nana's voice began to sound a little more animated.

He sat heavily in the orange vinyl chair. "Gracie Garcia. She runs a school teaching English as a Second Language and other skills to immigrants in the community. Her school sits where the pool was slated to go for the condo project. I knew I'd need a knockout punch to prove to the board I could do the CEO's job, so to ensure I could easily end the lease on that property and tear it down, I got Carter Porter to propose an ordinance at the City Council for Maximized Revenue Zones that would eliminate nonprofit businesses along Gulfview Boulevard."

Diana pressed a button and made the top of the bed sit up. "Jake, that sounds like a scheme your father would cook up."

"I know, Nana. I wanted to show the board I wasn't as bad a businessman as he said I was. But once I got to know Gracie, I saw her school filled a real need here and I learned she didn't have the funds to relocate. So, Friday night, I called Carter and told him to pull the plug on the vote. But he didn't and the proposal passed anyway. Her school will have to close. Her American dream is dead, and it's all my fault. I've lost my own business and I've killed Gracie's, too."

The first signs of color in days flushed over Nana's pale cheeks. "Jakey, Jenna and I talked briefly before you got back here from the cafeteria. It's about time I settle down and make some changes in my life. Maybe God's telling me retirement isn't the dirty word I always thought it would be." A full smile spread across her dry lips. "I need you to run an errand for me."

GRACIE SAT IN THE MIDDLE of her classroom. She didn't know if she would ever smile again. Her heart had fallen somewhere around her ankles at the sound of the mayor's gavel earlier. The three distinct thuds echoed constantly in her ears.

A knock at the door made Gracie jump. It sounded just like that stupid gavel. She peeked through the window instead of opening the door. Gracie didn't want to talk to anyone right now. She felt far too much self-pity to be good company.

Pastor Ruiz stood on the front porch. She couldn't be rude and pretend not to be home. He'd always treated her like a daughter.

"*Holá*, Gracie," he said as she pulled the door open. "Gloria called. She said you might need a sympathetic ear today."

She closed the door behind him. "I don't feel much like talking right now, Pastor."

"I understand. Maybe I could do the talking, then." He sat down on one of the chairs in the classroom.

Gracie pulled out a chair nearby and slumped into it. "I don't think there's anything you could say that would make my heart stop hurting, Pastor Ruiz."

"Do you remember the story of Jeremiah?"

She nodded. "He's a prophet from the Old Testament, right?" "Exactly. And much like what's happened to you now, Jeremiah didn't like the situation he found himself in. One day, God had him write a letter to the other exiles like him. In it, God reminded the people that even though they weren't living in their lands, He still had a plan for their lives."

Gracie straightened in her chair. "What are you trying to say?"

"Well, Gracie, God has brought you to this place, a long way from your homeland. You're here for a purpose." The pastor leaned forward, resting his hands on his knees. "I don't know what God has in store for you, but He hasn't forgotten you, and the work you've been doing is not in vain."

Slowly, she could feel her heart begin to inch back to its rightful place. "But what about Jake, Pastor? I trusted him. I've prayed about him, and this wasn't the way I thought it was supposed to work out."

"Trusting others isn't a bad thing, Graciela. But above all, you have to trust in God. Even when His timing is not our own."

Gracie knew Pastor Ruiz spoke the truth. "Easier said than done."

"Most of the important things in life are, *hija*." He reached out and gave her a reassuring pat on the knee. "I have some boxes in the church office. I'll go get them and then come back to help you start packing."

"Thanks, Pastor. I appreciate your stopping by." They both rose and walked back to the door.

"Anytime. I'll be back in an hour or so."

He opened the door and left Gracie standing in the front hallway, alone again with her thoughts.

Suddenly, Gracie felt very small. She'd been raised to have faith. But in the toughest afternoon of her life, she'd forgotten all about it. How could she rebuild on a foundation that proved to be so easily shaken?

Maybe some hot tea and quiet time with her Bible would do the trick. She began to walk down the hallway to the kitchen. An insistent knock on the door stopped her in her tracks.

"Gracie!"

She knew that voice. It haunted her thoughts.

Jake's fist connected with the door again.

"Gracie, please open the door. Your car is parked out front. I know you're here."

Every fiber of her body wanted to stay put. But Gracie knew she couldn't hide. Not from Jake or from whatever lay ahead in her now-uncertain path. She retraced her steps back to the door, then slowly turned the doorknob.

He looked as disheveled as he had at the hospital. His shirttail wasn't tucked in and his khaki shorts—the same ones he'd worn Saturday on the boat—were wrinkled almost beyond recognition. A dark stain marred the hemline on the right leg. She clearly wasn't the only one who had been dealt a one-two punch recently.

"Gracie. I have something for you." He stood on the porch, not pushing to come inside.

"I think you've given me enough, Jake." She didn't mean to be harsh. The words just came out of her mouth before she could think them through.

He held up a goldenrod-colored envelope, the size of a sheet of paper. "Take this. It's yours."

"But I didn't leave anything behind on Saturday." She took the envelope and held it gingerly, as though it would scorch what little she had left to her name.

"It's not from Saturday." His green eyes focused on her with the intensity of a bear trap. "Please open it."

A slight tremble ruffled her fingers as she tore the flap of the envelope. Inside rested two pieces of paper. One, a sheet from a yellow legal pad, the other a blue rectangle. Gracie pulled out the yellow page first.

A short paragraph was shakily handwritten in black ink. Gracie's voice faltered as she read aloud.

> Dear Ms. Garcia, It gives me great pleasure to award you a grant from the Peoples Family Foundation in the amount of $25,000. It is the foundation's hope that you will be able to continue your work educating the citizens of Port Provident in a new location and to begin your GED program. The foundation's new director, Jake Peoples, will be able to assist you should you have any further needs beyond this initial grant.
>
> Sincerely yours,
>
> Diana Powell Peoples.

Digging back in the envelope, Gracie found the blue rectangle. As the letter said, it was a check written in the sum of $25,000—$10,000 more than the grant she'd hoped to receive but hadn't.

Gracie tried to get a tight grip on her feelings, even as they began to take flight. She felt as if she was grasping at dangling strings from balloons rising on the breeze.

"What is this?"

"I had a heart-to-heart with Nana about what's happened the last few days—if you'll pardon the pun, considering why Nana's been in the hospital. The subject of you and me and *El Centro* came up. She reminded me that she and Jenna happen to be in charge of a foundation that makes charitable grants to worthy causes in the Port Provident community. But with

Jenna about to start a family and Nana recovering from her heart attack, there's a position open at the Peoples Family Foundation—and there's no board of directors and DNA isn't a job requirement." Jake cracked a smile. "She also asked that I apologize for the informal letter, but the nurses wouldn't let me bring her laptop into the ICU."

She scanned the letter again, still unable to believe she held a grant check in her hands. "So... you have a new job here in Port Provident after all?"

"One where I can work with people and help them achieve their dreams—just as you and I talked about on the boat. Just as my great-grandfather did after the hurricane."

Gracie leaned against the doorframe for support, overwhelmed. "Pastor Ruiz was right. God does have a plan, even when we can't see it. I don't know how to thank you—or Him."

"I have that praise and worship CD you accidentally left in my truck Wednesday night after church. He might like it if we drove down to the beach and sang along. We both have things to show our thanks for."

Gracie liked the sound of Jake's plan. Gratitude continued to wash over her with the repetitive force of one cresting wave after another.

"As for me," Jake said, taking one measured step in Gracie's direction, "I'd settle for a kiss. I want to know everything's okay between the two of us. We had a misunderstanding the last few days, but I had to tell you...I love you. I'm not some shallow, narrow-minded guy from your past. I want to be with you. Forever. Please don't ever question that."

Acting on pure emotion, Gracie leapt forward and threw her arms around Jake's neck. Together, she knew they could weather any storm life threw in their direction.

"Teacher?" Jake brought his head low to Gracie's ear.

"Yes?"

"How do you say I love you in Spanish? I seem to have forgotten."

His breath stirred her hair.

"*Te amo*," she whispered.

"*Te amo*, Graciela Garcia de Piedra. Remember that, *maestra*. There'll be a quiz later."

Epilogue

THE SUN SHONE BRIGHTLY for the ribbon-cutting at the new downtown location of *El Centro por las Lenguas*.

Gracie had spent the last two months fixing up the school and her loft upstairs. She not only had the Peoples Family Foundation grant money to work with—but getting to know Jake's grandmother opened doors to other prominent citizens of Port Provident, who generously made donations as well.

"Gracie, I want you to meet Dr. Gary Stone." Diana Peoples hadn't kept her vow to settle down after her heart attack. She used all her event-planning skills to make sure the school's opening was a success.

Gracie extended her hand. "It's a pleasure to meet you, Dr. Stone."

"The pleasure's all mine, Ms. Garcia. I've known Diana for years, and anyone she speaks this highly of has to be very special."

Gracie felt the mild heat of blushing creep into her cheeks at the unexpected compliment. She'd spent a great deal of time with the matriarch of the Peoples family during the past eight weeks. Gracie loved hearing that the affection she held for Jake's grandmother was mutual.

"Dr. Stone is the new president of Provident College, Gracie." Diana's friendly smile made Gracie feel as though she, too, belonged to this circle of friends.

"Welcome, Dr. Stone. Several students of mine have gone on to study at PC, and I myself attended several years ago."

Gracie loved that God had provided her with students from day one of opening *El Centro*, but she regretted that her difficulties with David kept her away from furthering her own education.

"But you aren't a graduate of our institution, correct?"

Gracie noticed a sheen of perspiration begin to pop up on the college president's brow as they stood in the afternoon sun.

"No, in addition to working full time, I haven't really had the money to pay for school."

Dr. Stone grinned. "Well, you do now. I'm here to provide you with a full-tuition scholarship to Provident College. When Diana told me about your school, as a fellow educator, I knew how important education had to be to you. I want you to have the same opportunity for advancement you provide your own students."

"Oh, *gracias*!" Excitement caused Gracie to slip into her native tongue.

Jake tugged at his *novia*'s elbow before she could say anything more. "I hate to interrupt, but everyone from the Chamber of Commerce is here. We should probably cut the ribbon so everyone can get inside to the air-conditioning. No one wants to stand outside in a Texas summer."

Gracie allowed Jake to lead her up to the front of the crowd. His strong arm around her waist kept her jitters at bay.

"Here are the scissors, Gracie." Laura Allen, the president of the Chamber of Commerce, handed over a pair of scissors the size of an elementary-school student.

Gracie felt as if she'd joined a clown skit in a circus. "Thank you, everyone, for coming today to celebrate the grand opening of the new location of *El Centro por las Lenguas*. Your support means so much to me."

Gracie turned and tried to hold the scissors in the least-awkward way possible. Her first attempt at cutting barely nicked the fluffy red bow.

"I think you need to get a little bit closer," Jake said as he gently pushed her forward. Gracie readied herself for another try. As she settled herself, the sunlight glinted off something in the ribbon.

"Hold these, please." She handed the scissors to Jake. "What is that?"

Standing next to the giant bow tied in front of her school's front door, Gracie noticed a small diamond ring tied to the top of the crimson loops.

"Jake? What is this?"

Her heart began to pound, giant thumps that had to be obvious to the gathered crowd.

Instead of replying, Jake dropped to one knee. "Before we cut the ribbon to start the next phase of your school, I want to start the next phase of your life. Graciela Garcia de Piedra, will you marry me?"

Gracie looked deep into Jake's eyes and saw an ocean of love in their depths. When she left her home in Mexico as a child, she could never have imagined this day. Tears as clear as the diamond before her ran down her cheeks.

Without hesitation, Gracie answered Jake with the language of her youth. "¡*Sí*!"

You Don't Have to Leave Port Provident!

Start Legacy of Love Now!

SAMANTHA SPAETH HAS spent her life conquering her fears. The Director of the Port Provident Historical Society isn't afraid of anything, except the fact that she is running out of time to save one of the island's most historic landmarks before it succumbs to development by a big-box store.

The black sheep of the island's oldest family, Whitt Peoples knows this Christmas will be the worst holiday in his life. The high-powered corporate consultant is used to saving dying companies, but he can't save his dying grandmother.

Returning to Port Provident for the first time since his childhood, he hopes to slip into town—and then leave as soon as possible—without running into the other side of his family who turned their back on him when he was a kid. Can a woman who lives for the lessons of the past use the town's heritage to bring the legacy of true love to a man who's spent his whole life running away?

https://books2read.com/LegacyOfLoveBook

Join Kristen's Reader Community Today and Receive a Free Port Provident Story

Join Kristen's reader community today for the latest and get A Place to Find Love, *a sweet escape romance that introduces you to Port Provident, Texas and the residents who find love on the island, for free!*
[*www.kristenethridge.com/newsletter*](http://www.kristenethridge.com/newsletter)[1]

Sneak Peek: Legacy of Love—Chapter One

WHITTEN PEOPLES STOOD on the raised wall that protected Provident Island from the ravages of nature's storms. Almost as soon as the scent of the coastal air hit his lungs, it didn't take long for Whitt to remember why he'd left town and had once vowed never to return.

Regret. It smelled like saltwater.

Unfortunately, it looked like Kaye Vontegarten. The phone call came through this morning and informed Whitt that his grandmother wasn't expected to make it through the night. He called his assistant and instructed her on what to book for his trip, then he packed a bag. When his plane from New York

---

City landed at Bush Intercontinental Airport in Houston, he rented a car for the drive south to the coast and Port Provident, Texas.

Whitt stuck his hands in his pockets, balling his fists and pressing against the seam beneath his knuckles. He struggled to move the crisp, yet-still-humid air past the lump in his throat. Granny couldn't be going. She was the only link he had to his mother. And now she—and the love and memories she'd so generously shared with him his whole life—would be gone, just as gone as his mother was.

This would be the worst Christmas ever. You were supposed to get presents at Christmas, not lose them. Granny had been the greatest gift in his life. And before the needles would fall off the trees in homes all over Port Provident...Granny would leave this world for the next.

"Did you know this was where the Port Provident Children's Home stood before the Great Storm of 1910?"

Whitt turned his head as a woman spoke softly next to him. Her voice rose just barely over the sound of the perpetual motion of the waves below.

"No, I didn't."

"Right there, across the street."

He knew he should have been friendlier. He should have had some kind of reply for her wistful commentary. But not today. Not while his grandmother lay confined in a regulation-style hospital bed a few blocks away. Whitt spent his life immersed in technology. He spent his days coaching the next round of tech entrepreneurs—he helped save fledgling businesses with good ideas. But none of it could save Granny.

It made his heart hurt.

In a way, that surprised him more than anything else that had happened today, because Whitt Peoples was almost sure he didn't have a heart anymore.

"Do you live here?" The quiet voice asked another question.

"No, just visiting."

She pulled out a slick, colorful piece of paper, carefully folded into a narrow rectangle. "I'm Samantha Spaeth with the Port Provident Historical Society. We're dedicating a new exhibit at our Port Provident Historical Museum to the Children's Home and the heroism the night of the Great Storm of 1910."

Whitt took the folded paper and stuffed it in his pocket without more than a passing glance. "Y'all sure talk about the Great Storm a lot around here, don't you?" Whitt had spent the first ten years of his life on Provident Island. Then he moved to the city that never sleeps. From all appearances, Port Provident was still taking a nap, still stuck in the past.

"Hurricanes are a way of life here on the coast, Mr..."

Whitt could hear the question in her voice as the end of her sentence trailed off. Maybe if he answered her and played along for a moment, she'd leave him alone with the rest of his thoughts. A hundred meaningless dinner parties in New York's dining rooms and hotels had prepared him for moments like this.

"Peoples. Whitt Peoples. Nice to meet you, Ms. Spaeth."

It wasn't, but he'd do or say just about anything right now in order to be left alone for the few minutes he needed to compose himself before he went to Granny's bedside.

"Peoples? Are you related to Diana Peoples, by chance?"

Whitt nodded shortly. He'd intended to play a game, but not Twenty Questions.

"My grandmother."

A smile like a Gulf of Mexico sunrise spread across Samantha Spaeth's island-tanned face. "But you said you were just visiting."

"I am. I live in New York City now."

The glow continued to warm her features. "Well, you should come tomorrow, Mr. Peoples. We're honoring John Peoples as part of the exhibit."

A seagull squawked loudly from a weathered post that had been stuck out a dozen feet beyond the shoreline. Whitt knew precisely how the bird felt. He wanted to squawk and flap this woman away. "Who?"

"John Peoples, your great-grandfather!"

She practically squealed. Whitt sharply eyed the seagull on the post, trying telepathically to convince him to fly over here. Maybe he could flap his wings and scare the historical cheerleader off.

"Never knew him." Whitt looked at his watch. Ten more minutes until he had planned to check in on the one grandmother who still mattered to him.

"Of course not. He died several decades ago." She held out another brochure and pointed at a photo on the front. "But Diana and some other members of your family will be there. It would be an honor to have you there with them."

He could respond to her enthusiasm truthfully—and look like a total loser. But not only did he not have any idea who John Peoples was, he didn't know Diana well. Nor did he really know any of the other members of the Peoples family still here in Port Provident.

And—he didn't really care to. It wasn't like they'd followed up with him after he and his dad moved away from Port Provident when Whitt was ten. They hadn't cared about having him in their life. Why should he care about being in theirs?

The only person he cared about on Provident Island was dying in ICU. He wasn't about to waste time shaking hands and giving air kisses to people he hadn't seen in more than twenty years.

Honesty was the best policy.

If Whitt told her why he was really here, she'd feel sorry for him and leave him alone. That's what strangers did. They went away when things got uncomfortable.

Well, strangers and most members of the Peoples family.

"I'm afraid I'm only here for a few days. I've come because of a death in the family. In fact, I need to take care of a few things."

"Oh, I'm so sorry."

"It's okay." Another lie, but he didn't care. He'd save truth—all of it—for his grandmother. That's what final goodbyes were for.

And on that note, it was time to say goodbye to the blonde stranger next to him. At another time, in another place, he might have bought her a drink, might have asked her some stupid pick-up-line questions. But not now. Not today.

He felt the brochure bend between his fingers and noticed there was a trash can up ahead. If he could get far enough down the sidewalk on Gulfview Boulevard, it would make the chances of her seeing him dumping her invitation to the museum-based Peoples family reunion very slim. Whitt had absolutely no intentions of attending tomorrow's highlight of the Port Provident holiday social season, but he also didn't want to hurt the poor woman's feelings. After all, he figured she wouldn't be outside on a sidewalk above the Gulf of Mexico in the week before Christmas handing brochures to passers-by if she didn't care deeply about her job and the event.

Granny had always reminded him to think about the impacts of his actions on others—even the small gestures. It had been good advice.

He couldn't keep his thoughts off Granny and the life lessons she'd always tried to instill in him. The knowledge that most likely, after tonight, there'd be no more soft-spoken wisdom from her lips and her heart...well, the harsh thought leveled on him like a weight the size of Texas.

A gust of December sea breeze blew in as Whitt picked up his small bag and walked down the sidewalk at the edge of the Gulf. Having lived in New York for twenty years, Whitt never would have believed a winter breeze on a Texas island could chill him to the bone.

But at this moment, he felt colder than he ever had in his life.

He knew it wasn't the wind.

SAMANTHA DROPPED THE last stack of brochures on the counter at Café Provident, the island's favorite coffee shop. Located in the heart of Port Provident's historic downtown shopping area, the artistic café was popular with locals and received plenty of foot traffic from tourists out shopping for the holidays. Samantha needed to finish her mission strong by grabbing as much attention of both groups as she could in the next twenty-four hours.

One of the museum's board members had pulled a few strings and secured national journalist Reid Knight to come and report on the museum and the Great Storm for his new show, America's Small Town Surprises. The show was about to launch on HSH, the Home Sweet Home network and the first episode would feature Port Provident. Samantha knew it was critical that they have a good turnout and showcase the city, as well as Port Provident's unique history.

"Hey this looks promising," Samantha said as she arranged the slick paper next to the cash register. "All the brochures I put out last week are gone. Has anyone said anything about coming? Any chit-chat while people are waiting at the counter?"

Beth Greenling, the owner of Café Provident, finished a transaction at the register and handed a receipt to a customer with a smile, then turned toward Samantha.

"A few have. Becca from the animal shelter was in here over the weekend, and she said has it on the calendar."

Samantha smiled. "I wonder what happened to all the animals that night. I can't even imagine the chaos. People had to be just sick about making choices about keeping themselves and their children alive. I wouldn't think there would be much time to help the pets too. So sad."

Beth nodded. "I think I would have been terrified. I'm glad the Gulf was quiet this past summer. I read a report that they're predicting a more active season next year—I really hope that doesn't come to pass. But I'm always fascinated by the stories that come out of disasters—you get to see that there are heroes around every corner."

"Which is exactly the point of this new exhibit. Without John Peoples' leadership, Port Provident likely wouldn't have been rebuilt. And without his heroism the night of the storm, well, Isabel Schuster and Ingrid Buchholz wouldn't have been saved, and there would have been no one to tell the story of the Children's Home—there would have been no connection to remember those innocent lives."

Beth stirred a splash of milk into Samantha's coffee. "You know, I moved here to get away from corporate America, to leave the rat race behind. I wanted to disconnect and look at the beach every day—you know, enjoy the solitude and doing my own thing. But I think I'm more connected than ever. I love this community. I love the people of Port Provident and the history that's happened here over the years and how it still shapes and defines this city, even today."

"Oh, me too." Samantha inhaled the scent of the warm, roasted beans that filled Café Provident. "When I had the chance to come work here, I hadn't grown up that far away, so I knew about the Great Storm, but I didn't know much else. I mainly came for the beach."

Samantha took a cautious sip of the hot coffee Beth had handed her. "But during the last few years, I've learned so much about this place. I haven't just learned the history, I've gotten involved at First Provident Church, and I've made some true friends—which, in turn, means I've learned a lot about myself. You know, working on this Children's Home project has been freeing. It's like there are no secrets anymore about this huge part of the city's history. I like that—we're unearthing the surprises of history at the center. I'm the girl who never even wanted surprise parties as a kid."

"No surprise parties? Oh, boo. Where's the fun in that, Sam?" Beth handed her friend two bills and some coins in change.

"Order. Detail. Being prepared. It's a great feeling. Now, I need to get enough people to come so we make a splash on that TV show. I've got all my fingers crossed—I've just gotta keep hustling for the next few hours."

"Pfft."

Samantha heard a forceful hiss from the doorway of the café.

"Crossing fingers will only get you a hand cramp. I wish someone could explain the point of walking around with twisted fingers. Don't people pray anymore?"

The bell overhead jingled as Diana Peoples, town matriarch and benefactor of the Port Provident Historical Society, walked through Café Provident's door.

"Ha. I knew you'd say that, Diana." Samantha smiled. During the past year as she'd worked on this exhibit, Diana had become a friend and mentor—almost like a grandmother. She was full of advice and wisdom and knew more about the people and history of Port Provident than nearly anyone else Samantha had met on Provident Island.

The thought of people she'd met triggered an idea in Sam's mind. "I met someone today who said he knows you."

Diana brightened the winter day with the warmth of her smile. "Well, that's the bonus of living your whole life in one place...you get to know lots of people. Who was it?"

"Whitten Peoples. He said he was your grandson, and he was just in town for a few days because of a death in the family. So, he couldn't make it to the event tomorrow. If something's going on and you can't make it either, just let me know."

Diana took a slight step backward. If Samantha hadn't been making eye contact as they spoke, she never would have noticed.

The color fell from Diana's cheeks like the unusual snowfall the island had seen last Christmas.

"Whitt is here?"

Samantha nodded. "That's what he said his name was. He was about six-foot-two and had dark brown hair and dark brown eyes. Sound about right?"

The older woman nodded briefly and made a general noise of agreement. "*Mmhmm.* I...um, I guess so, yes."

The end of Diana's sentence came out strong, but Samantha had noticed her initial struggle for words. Something wasn't adding up.

"Beth, can I get my latte to go?"

Diana was a regular at Café Provident, and Beth knew what her regulars liked. She'd started preparing her order as soon as Diana walked through the door.

"Of course, Diana. Here." Beth pushed a white lid tightly around the rim of the cup and handed it to Diana. "It'll be four-seventy-nine."

Diana held the cup in one hand and dug in her designer brown leather purse. Her movements were jerky. "Here you go. Keep the change, dear."

She leaned forward and put a twenty-dollar bill on the counter and then turned and walked out the door without saying another word.

"Well, that's a first," Beth said as she counted out the change and dropped it into the tip jar. The coins made a loud clink as they came to rest on the rest of the day's gratuities. "I have never seen Diana Peoples just leave. She always says goodbye. Do you think everything's okay?"

"I don't know." Samantha looked out the window and watched Diana's car until it turned at the end of the block. "It was like she saw a ghost."

WHITT STOOD OUTSIDE the door to Granny's assigned room at Provident Medical Center. The steady beeps from the machines did nothing to steady his anxiety about what was going on within the tiny quarters.

"Mr. Peoples?" An older man in a white coat stopped alongside Whitt. "I'm Dr. Carlson. The nurses told me you were here. They'll have some paperwork for you to go over in a bit, but first, let me update you on Mrs. Vontegarten's condition."

Dr. Carlson spoke in clinical terms, giving Whitt a summary of his grandmother's condition. Whitt heard none of it. Instead, he watched the nurse swap out the IV bag that attached to the tubing in the frail hand. She made a few small adjustments, then peeled off the tape that held the IV in place. Patting Granny's hand gently, the nurse said something to her, then affixed another strip of tape to hold the tubing in place.

"Jeannie's a good nurse. She takes good care of her patients. Mrs. Vontegarten doesn't know what she's saying, but Jeannie treats everyone the same."

Whitt turned away from the scene in the room. "What do you mean Granny doesn't understand the nurse?"

"Well, she may technically be able to hear Jeannie, but your grandmother's been unresponsive for the last thirty-six hours or so. It's perfectly normal at this stage."

Whitt felt his heart break, like a fall leaf crushed in the palm of a child's hand. He noticed the pop and crackle as the curves flattened, as though nothing would ever be the same again.

Another nurse tapped Dr. Carlson on the shoulder and showed him a piece of paper. "I'll be back to check on her later this evening, Mr. Peoples."

Whitt nodded. It was all he could do.

He stood there, feet rooted to the heavy-duty vinyl tiles of the hospital hallway. He watched Jeannie adjust Granny's pillows and remembered crawling into a big four-poster bed the night his mother died.

Whitt rolled from his side to his stomach, unable to stop the tears. He pressed his face hard into the pillow. He smelled dust and feathers and the faintest hint of floral-scented laundry detergent.

He wanted to be with her, to go with her.

He was eight, and his world had just ended, washed away on a flood of tears.

Today in school, he'd presented his report on what he wanted to be when he grew up. Now, none of it mattered. He didn't want to grow up in a world without Mommy.

A gentle hand rubbed his back in a circle, smoothing the cotton of his T-shirt.

Sssh, she said, over and over. Sssh.

"I want to go with her too." She laid down beside him and wrapped him in her arms. "She's with the angels now. We'll see her again, Whitt. We'll see her again. But for now, we need to rest. We need to rest, and while we do, she'll still be with us in our dreams."

Jeannie crooked her finger and indicated for Whitt to come inside the room.

It broke the train of his memories, but soon all memories would be what Whitt had left.

He sighed. It hurt.

"She's resting comfortably, Mr. Peoples."

Whitt nodded. "I saw you taking good care of her. Thank you."

"Oh, Miss Kaye and I are old friends. I can't let her down." She beamed, then looked down at the bed-ridden woman and gave her hand a light squeeze.

"You know Granny?"

"Oh sure. I sing in the choir at First Provident. Even after she stopped being able to drive, Miss Kaye always made sure someone picked her up and brought her to church. She'd never miss a Sunday."

Whitt looked down at the thin frame under the white hospital sheet. Granny had changed so much since the last time he'd seen her.

Apparently, she'd changed in more ways than one.

"I only heard her talk about angels once in my life. I didn't know she went to church."

"She did. And we all loved her." The smile never left Jeannie's face. "I've got paperwork for you to sign, Mr. Peoples. She signed a Do Not Resuscitate order when she came in and gave us a Durable Power of Attorney with your name on it. I think she wanted to make things as easy on you as possible."

He watched the rise and fall of her chest, in time with the machines. "What does that mean?"

"It means that you're authorized to make healthcare decisions on her behalf, but that she does not want extraordinary measures taken to prolong her life. So, if she goes into cardiac arrest, I won't be getting a crash cart. She wants us to let her go."

"Go." The word popped out of Whitt's mouth, like the nurse was speaking a foreign language. The syllable felt dry and unfamiliar. "She wants to go."

"She hasn't been communicative for about three days, but when she was still in and out, she said she missed Julie."

He felt the saltwater of tears shed long ago prick at his eyes again. He breathed out and touched Granny's right hand. "I do, too."

Jeannie said nothing further, just patted him lightly on the shoulder as she passed.

Whitt felt the vellum-thin skin covering the back of Kaye's hand. The time between beeps seemed to linger. The nurse had said Granny tried to make this as easy as possible, but nothing would make this transition easy on Whitt.

His mother was gone. He hadn't really spoken to his father in years, except for surface conversations. They mostly communicated in short, periodic text messages. Even a random blonde stranger on Gulfview Boulevard knew more about his family than he did.

When the beeps stopped announcing the slowing march of Kaye Vontegarten's vital signs, when there was only silence to surround him instead of his granny's tight embrace...Whitt would be alone.

He'd spent his whole life pretending like flying solo was okay. He'd always been one to act tough and independent.

But deep down inside, where his heart tried to match the ebbing rhythm of the one in front of him, he knew it wasn't.

Keep reading Legacy of Love
Click here: https://books2read.com/LegacyOfLoveBook

Want to extend your stay in Port Provident?
Start a new book now!
The Home to Love Series
Language of Love[2]
Legacy of Love[3]
Labor of Love[4]
The Holiday Hearts Series

---

2. https://books2read.com/LanguageOfLoveBook

3. https://books2read.com/LegacyOfLoveBook

4. https://books2read.com/LaborOfLove

The Right Resolution[5]
The Cupid Caper[6]
Lucky in Love[7]
May I Have This Dance[8]
First Kiss Fireworks[9]
Falling Forever This Time[10]
Thankful for Love[11]
Mission: Mistletoe[12]
The Hope and Hearts Series
Shelter from the Storm[13]
The Doctor's Unexpected Family[14]
His Texas Princess[15]
Holiday of Hope[16]

Other Books by Kristen

Love Hallmark movies? Pick up Kristen's book October Kiss, based on the Hallmark movie viewers love! Available anywhere books are sold—in paperback, digital, and audio! October Kiss from Hallmark Publishing[17]

5. http://www.books2read.com/TheRightResolutionBook

6. http://www.books2read.com/TheCupidCaperBook

7. http://www.books2read.com/LuckyInLoveBook

8. http://www.books2read.com/MayIHaveThisDanceBook

9. http://www.books2read.com/FirstKissFireworksBook

10. http://www.books2read.com/FallingForeverThisTimeBook

11. http://www.books2read.com/ThankfulForLoveBook

12. http://www.books2read.com/MissionMistletoeBook

13. http://www.books2read.com/ShelterFromTheStorm

14. http://www.books2read.com/TheDoctorsUnexpectedFamily

15. http://www.books2read.com/HisTexasPrincess

16. http://www.books2read.com/HolidayOfHope

About Kristen

USA TODAY BESTSELLING Author Kristen Ethridge loves watching waves at the beach, eating the perfect taco, and reading books that leave her with a smile. Some would say her superpower is keeping alive one husband, three children, and six guinea pigs during their adventures across Texas—but that's not entirely true. She actually earned her sparkly cape for writing her signature style of Sweet Escape Romances—stories with hope, heart and happily-ever-after—for Harlequin's Love Inspired line, Hallmark Publishing, and Laurel Lock Publishing. One reader (who wasn't her mother) called Kristen's books "very good escape fiction" and that's pretty much the nicest thing anyone's ever said to her.

Kristen always wants to make new book best friends. Receive an exclusive free story by joining her mailing list at www.kristenethridge.com/newsletter. You can also follow her adventures in writing at www.facebook.com/kristenethridgebooks[1].

Keep up with Kristen through her author pages on Bookbub[2] and Facebook[3]. If you can't get enough of Port Provident, come join the Port Provident Community Center[4] on Facebook, the official gathering place for Kristen and her fans.

www.kristenethridge.com[5]
Facebook[6] Instagram[7]
The Port Provident Community[8] Center
Don't forget...if you love sweet escape romances, join Kristen's newsletter[9]!

1.   http://www.facebook.com/kristenethridgebooks

2.   https://www.bookbub.com/authors/kristen-ethridge

3.   http://www.facebook.com/kristenethridgebooks

4.   https://www.facebook.com/groups/2422381554654795

5. http://www.kristenethridge.com

6. https://www.facebook.com/KristenEthridgeBooks

7. https://instagram.com/kristenethridge

8. https://www.facebook.com/groups/2422381554654795

9. http://www.kristenethridge.com

LAUREL LOCK PUBLISHING

Publisher's Note: This is a work of fiction. Names, characters, places, and incidents are a product of the author's imagination. Locales and public names are sometimes used for atmospheric purposes. Any resemblance to actual people, living or dead, or to businesses, companies, events, institutions, or locales is completely coincidental.

Scriptures taken from the Holy Bible, New International Version®, NIV®. Copyright © 1973, 1978, 1984, 2011 by Biblica, Inc.™ Used by permission of Zondervan. All rights reserved worldwide. www.zondervan.com[10] The "NIV" and "New International Version" are trademarks registered in the United States Patent and Trademark Office by Biblica, Inc.™

Book Layout ©2013 BookDesignTemplates.com